It was all tot
She'd worked
two years, bu
case like this

Why did it matter how many times the man had gone diving, whether the water had been cold or what the currents had been like? Obviously the questions carried some significance or presumably Alex wouldn't be asking them. She was fascinated, and dying to know more, but she didn't like to question him while the patient was listening. Besides, she didn't feel they'd established any sort of professional relationship yet. She didn't feel comfortable asking questions.

She hadn't managed to separate Alex the doctor from Alex the seducer.

Dear Reader

I've wanted to write a book about triplets for a long time, so when my editor suggested a trilogy I knew instantly how the books would be linked. It's fascinating to observe the differences between children from the same family, and my triplets are no exception.

First we have **Katy**—she's cool and reserved on the surface, but underneath she has a wildly passionate nature that's been repressed to suit the conservative expectations of her wealthy, aristocratic family. Only one man knows the real Katy, and he's about to walk back into her life…

Then there's **Libby**—she's free spirited and independent and has attitude by the bucket-load. It's going to take a strong man to attract her attention, and he's about to buy her in an auction…

And finally their brother **Alex.** Alex is a skilled A&E doctor, and so sinfully sexy and eligible that women can't resist him. But he isn't interested in commitment—until he meets Jenny and his well-ordered bachelor existence is turned upside down.

Two sisters and a brother, all different but linked by a powerful emotional bond, each finding love in different ways. They are the Westerling triplets, and I hope you enjoy getting to know them.

Warmly,

Sarah

THE ENGLISH DOCTOR'S BABY

BY
SARAH MORGAN

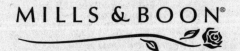

First published in Great Britain 2004
Harlequin Mills & Boon Limited,
Eton House, 18-24 Paradise Road, Richmond, Surrey TW9 1SR

© Sarah Morgan 2004

ISBN 0 263 83897 8

Set in Times Roman 10½ on 11¼ pt.
03-0504-59115

Printed and bound in Spain
by Litografia Rosés, S.A., Barcelona

CHAPTER ONE

'WE'VE arrived, sweetheart.' Jenny switched off the engine. Her mouth was dry and her heart was banging against her ribs so hard that she felt dizzy. 'Get ready to meet your daddy.'

She closed her eyes briefly and then turned to look at the baby, safely strapped in a car seat next to her.

Was she doing the right thing?

She'd ached over the decision for months and now the moment had finally come she was suddenly filled with doubt.

Was Alex Westerling really the right father for an innocent baby?

The answer had to be no.

But what choice did she have?

She brushed the baby's cheek with a gentle finger. 'You do realise that I don't want to do this, don't you? He might be a doctor, but the man has a wicked reputation with women and he's never made a commitment to anyone in his life. The last thing I want to do is introduce him to *you*.' She broke off and nibbled her lip, worry creasing her brow. 'But I just can't see any other way. We need help. We can't manage on our own any more. And you need to know your daddy. It's time Alex Westerling lived up to his responsibilities.'

The baby cooed happily and kicked her legs.

Jenny gave a soft smile. 'Daisy Phillips, you are a beautiful baby. Let's just hope he thinks so too.'

But she wasn't optimistic.

From what she'd heard and read about Alex Westerling, babies, however beautiful, were not on his agenda. The only females who interested him were well over the age of consent.

According to gossip he was a super-cool, rich playboy who moved smoothly through life, leaving a trail of broken hearts littered behind him, and Jenny had absolutely no doubt that the reception awaiting her was going to be decidedly chilly.

Delaying the moment when she would have to leave the car, she turned to look out of the window, her eyes resting on the sea sparkling in the sun. It was a beautiful day. And she'd never felt more stressed in her life.

She absolutely loathed confrontation and you didn't have to be a genius to work out that she was about to get confrontation by the bucketload.

Alex Westerling was *not* going to be pleased to see her.

'Come on. Let's get it over with.' She gritted her teeth and stared down at the row of fishermen's cottages that backed onto the sand dunes. 'At least the man has taste. He lives in a nice place. Right by the beach. You'll like it when you're a bit older.'

Jenny opened her door and walked round the car. Daisy was still blowing bubbles as she undid the straps and lifted the baby carefully out of the seat and onto her shoulder.

Then she took a deep breath, locked the car and paused at the top of the path. 'Brace yourself, Alex Westerling,' she muttered, her hand shaking slightly as she stroked the baby's back. 'Your past is about to catch up with you.'

Three miles away in the accident and emergency department, Alex Westerling finished his examination and straightened up.

'Well? Am I done for, Doctor?' The elderly lady lying on the trolley scowled at him, but he saw the anxiety in her eyes.

'You're not done for, Mavis,' he said gently, replacing the blanket and lifting the sides of the trolley. 'But you won't be dancing for a few weeks. You've broken your ankle.'

'Broken my—' The old lady broke off and frowned. 'Nonsense. It's just sprained.'

'It's broken.'

'You can't know that. You haven't even sent me for an X-ray.'

'I'm going to do that now,' Alex replied, reaching for the appropriate form and scribbling on it. 'But I already know it's broken.'

'How? Are you Superman? Do doctors come equipped with X-ray vision these days?'

Alex handed the form to the staff nurse who was hovering. 'Mavis, you couldn't put any weight on it after you fell and you're tender over the medial malleolus—which is this bone here…' He lifted his trouser leg to show her on himself and she winked at him.

'Nice legs.'

Alex laughed and released his trouser leg. 'Glad you think so.'

'So if you're so clever, why are you bothering with the X-ray?'

'Because I want to have a proper look at the fracture,' he said patiently. 'Check that there isn't anything else I should know about. Do you want me to blind you with science? I can explain exactly what I'm looking for if you like. Talar shift, or—'

'All right, all right, I get the picture. I'll have the X-ray.' Mavis studied him carefully. 'I know you. You're the one that's always in those glossy magazines. Rolling in money. Son of Sir-something-or-other and Lady-something-or-other. They live in a stately home. I saw pictures of it in a magazine. Garden bigger than a park.'

The nurse froze and glanced nervously at Alex. Alex Westerling was notoriously close-mouthed about his personal life and his family connections and certainly no one who worked with him ever dared raise the subject.

There was a moment's tense silence and then Alex shook his head and started to laugh.

'Anything else you know about me, Mavis?'

'Only that you're a bit of a heartbreaker, if the reports are to be believed.'

'They're not,' Alex said dryly, and her eyes twinkled.

'I saw you last winter, didn't I? When I did my hip. I never forget a face. Especially when it's as good-looking as yours.'

'And I never forget a hip. I suppose you were running away from a man at the time,' Alex drawled lightly. 'Perhaps you'd better just stand still and let them catch you. That way you might stop breaking things.'

'Well, if it was you chasing me, I probably would,' the old lady returned. 'You're a handsome devil. It's almost worth breaking something just to bump into you again.'

Alex was visibly amused by his patient and the nurse relaxed. 'Do me a favour, Mavis. Next time you want my company just lift up the phone and we'll meet for a cup of tea or something. It's much simpler than breaking bones.'

'You saucy man! I'm eighty-six! Are you asking me out?'

'Maybe.' His blue eyes twinkled. 'But it's only fair to warn you that I don't do commitment.'

Mavis laughed with delight. 'At my age, who cares? I just want to be a bit wicked and have fun.'

Alex smiled. 'You're my kind of woman, Mavis.' His gaze flickered to the nurse who was still hovering. 'Can you arrange for someone to take her to X-ray, please, and then call me as soon as you have the films. I don't want her hanging around.'

'Oh—aren't you going to leave me waiting for twenty-four hours in a draughty corridor? You hear such dreadful things about accident departments these days,' Mavis said, and Alex slipped his pen back into his pocket.

'Not about my department. I'll see you later. Try not to shock anyone in X-ray or have any more accidents on the way.' He strolled out of the room and bumped into one of the A and E sisters, carrying a stack of X-rays. 'Any of those for me?'

Tina shook her head. 'Don't think so. You've been trapped with that RTA for most of the day so everyone else has been doing your work.'

Alex lifted an eyebrow. 'So if I've had such a slack day, how come I feel exhausted?'

Tina wrinkled her nose. 'Because you were up all night and only had two hours' sleep at your desk this morning?'

Alex rolled his eyes. 'That could have something to do with it. We either need more staff or fewer patients. There's definitely an imbalance somewhere.'

'So are you off home now?'

'As soon as I've checked Mavis Belling's X-rays.'

'Oh, no!' Tina looked dismayed. 'Is the poor thing in again? What is it this time?'

'Ankle.' Alex ran a hand over his jaw and noted that he needed a shave. 'Not as bad as last time, though. But I want to check her myself.'

Tina's eyes were soft. 'Has anyone ever told you you're a nice man, Alex Westerling?'

'Funnily enough, no,' Alex drawled. 'In fact, I'm usually being told the complete opposite.'

'Well, perhaps I should have said that you're a nice man at work. In your personal life you are definitely not so nice.' Tina's eyes twinkled merrily. 'You are very careless with female hearts.'

Alex yawned. 'Don't you start. I've just had Mavis reading my press cuttings.'

'Well, there are rather a lot of them,' Tina pointed out mildly, and he gave a careless shrug.

'Is it my fault if the press have nothing better to do than follow me around? Now, give me a break, Tina. I've been awake for the best part of thirty-six hours with this RTA. I don't need a lecture.'

He strolled to his office to catch up on some paperwork and stayed there, trying not to fall asleep at his desk until one of the nurses called him to tell him that Mavis was back.

He removed the X-rays from the packet and examined them one by one.

'Well, that could be worse. See this?' He tapped on the X-ray with his pen. 'You've got a lateral malleolar fracture but fortunately it's undisplaced.'

'Why fortunately?'

'Because you don't need an operation.' Alex flicked off the light-box. 'You need a below-knee plaster, some pain-killers and then you need to keep this leg elevated. I'm going to refer you to the orthopaedic surgeons for follow-up. You'll like them. They're a good-looking bunch. Be gentle with them.'

Mavis beamed. 'And will I see you again?'

'Not unless you break something else,' Alex said, scrib-bling a referral letter while he talked. 'Now, how are you going to manage at home with that leg in plaster?'

'Are you offering to come and bath me?'

Alex laughed. 'You're wicked, Mavis. What I had in mind was something rather more conventional, like the dis-trict nurse or perhaps a care assistant for a short time until you're fully mobile again.'

Mavis pulled a face. 'How boring.'

'But practical. I'll scribble a letter to your GP. He needs to check out your bones, if he hasn't already done so.'

He made the necessary arrangements, picked up his car keys and his jacket from his office and strolled towards his car.

It had been a rough ten days and he was starting to feel

the strain. Thank goodness there was only one more day to go before the weekend. He was going to spend the whole time sleeping and surfing.

No responsibilities.

He wasn't home.

Jenny tried the bell one more time and then stepped back and looked at the house. It wasn't what she'd expected. She knew that Alex Westerling was wealthy beyond her wildest imaginings and she'd assumed that his house would reflect his flashy lifestyle. But it didn't seem to. From the outside it looked like an ordinary fisherman's cottage.

She was trying to work out what that said about him when she heard the growl of a powerful engine approaching.

Every muscle in her body tensed and her heart took off at an indecent pace.

All her instincts warned her that it was *him* and the minute the low black sports car roared into view, she knew she was right.

If the house had been a surprise then the car was everything she'd expected and more. A sleek, blatant declaration of masculine self-indulgence that reflected everything she'd heard about his playboy tastes. Only someone as superficial as him would spend so much money on a lump of metal, she reflected as he turned into the drive and came to a smooth stop.

Jenny dragged some air into her lungs and clutched Daisy against her, taking reassurance from her solid warmth.

Now that the moment had finally come, she felt breathless with panic.

Whatever had possessed her to come here? What madness had made her think that confronting Alex Westerling was a good idea?

Suddenly she felt like running but her legs were wobbling so badly that she couldn't have moved even if there'd been anywhere to run to. And there wasn't. He was blocking the only exit.

Moving at a leisurely pace that served to intensify her anxiety, the driver stepped out of the car and removed his sunglasses. And for the first time in her life, Jenny set eyes on Alex Westerling.

She stared at him stupidly.

She'd seen pictures, of course. He was one of the Westerling triplets and she'd seen his picture everywhere, along with those of his two sisters, and because she'd seen his picture so often she'd assumed that she knew exactly what he looked like. But she realised now that she'd somehow managed to merge the pictures with her own contempt for the man and in the process had managed to distort the truth.

And the truth was that the man standing in front of her was the embodiment of all the most extreme female fantasies.

The sudden increase in her heart rate came as an unpleasant shock.

Handsome didn't begin to describe him. She'd met handsome men before and none of them had had the physical impact of Alex Westerling. Everything about him was exaggerated perfection—his shoulders were unreasonably broad, his eyes a startling blue and his bone structure more striking than any she'd seen before.

He was achingly, spectacularly good-looking—if you liked arrogant, powerful men who thought they owned the world, Jenny told herself quickly, trying to get her reaction under control.

He might be good-looking but he was still the heartless man who'd ruined her sister's life.

And for the first time she was beginning to see how it could have happened. How her sister could have been led to behave in such a wanton and impulsive way. It wasn't just his immense wealth and aristocratic connections that set Alex Westerling apart from other men—it was the raw, almost untamed masculinity that surrounded him like a cloak, an aura of power strong enough to make the most worldly of women act irrationally—and Chloe had certainly not been worldly.

He locked the car with a flick of his wrist and strolled towards her, his jacket slung casually over one broad shoulder.

Brilliant blue eyes focused on Jenny without a flicker of interest, as if he was totally accustomed to having strange females holding babies waiting on his doorstep.

Jenny felt her knees shake. She was hopeless with men like him. She never knew what to say and felt totally out of her depth. Alex Westerling was someone who mixed with models and actresses on a regular basis and she knew he wasn't going to waste a second glance on a plain, flat-chested mouse like her.

He paused in front of her, well over six feet two of raw male power. 'Presumably you're lost,' he drawled, his tone maddeningly indifferent. 'You should have carried straight on at the top of the road. This is a dead end. It doesn't lead anywhere.'

She forced herself to meet his gaze, reminding herself that this was about Daisy, not her.

Her voice was clear and steady as she spoke. 'It leads to you, Dr Westerling.'

The ensuing silence pulsed with tension and his gaze hardened.

'In that case I probably ought to remind you that this is my home and it's the one place in the world that I won't tolerate being pestered by journalists.'

The wobble in her knees intensified and she felt the courage ooze out of her.

She couldn't do this. She just couldn't do this.

He had an air of self-possession and unshakable cool that was thoroughly intimidating and if she had been a journalist she would have run a mile. No story would have been worth the cold, disdainful look that Alex Westerling was casting in her direction.

But she wasn't a journalist and as if to remind her of the reason for her presence, the baby lifted a hand and patted her cheek with a chubby hand.

Daisy.

That was why she was here, facing this man.

That innocent touch gave her the courage she needed and she lifted her chin and forced herself to meet his icy gaze. 'I'm not a reporter.'

His eyes swept over her dismissively. 'I've been awake for the best part of thirty-six hours and I'm not in the best of tempers,' he warned softly. 'Perhaps you could just tell me what it is you want and we can both get on with the rest of the day. Your baby looks tired.'

'She isn't my baby, Dr Westerling,' Jenny croaked, wondering how it was possible to shiver even in the height of summer, 'she's *your* baby. You're her father.'

CHAPTER TWO

THE silence stretched into infinity.

Alex stared at the petite, dark-haired girl in front of him and wished he'd managed to snatch more sleep at the hospital. His usually sharp mind seemed to have ground to a halt.

The girl cleared her throat again and his eyes followed the direction of the sound, noticing a pulse beating in her throat, registering that she was nervous.

In fact, she looked terrified.

Somehow he found that comforting.

If she was nervous then there had to be a reason and the most obvious reason was that she was lying. She had to be lying. For a start she wasn't his type. She was dark-haired and he knew for a fact he'd never had a relationship with someone of her colouring. His sisters delighted in teasing him about the fact that he always had a blonde on his arm. And then there was her manner. All the women he dated were confident and flirtatious whereas this girl was obviously using iron determination to stop herself from running.

His absolute conviction that they'd never had a relationship gave him comfort.

'Perhaps we should go inside to talk about this,' she suggested, and he shook his head.

As far as he was concerned, the only place she was going was back where she came from.

'What is there to talk about?'

She bristled angrily and he saw her dark eyes flash slightly as she clutched the baby more tightly.

He hid his surprise. Maybe she wasn't quite as placid and gentle as she'd first seemed.

She was glaring at him. 'That is exactly the type of comment I'd expect from a man like you.'

'A man like me?' He lifted an eyebrow. 'And you are, of course, intimately acquainted with me.'

He knew definitely that she wasn't and the fact that she blushed deeply merely confirmed it.

She chewed her lip. 'Well, no, but—'

'We're not intimately acquainted?' Alex's tone was mocking. 'And yet you're claiming that we slept together. Maybe your definition of intimate is different to mine.'

She pushed her dark hair away from her face with a shaking hand. 'We didn't sleep together.' She stumbled over the words as if she was uncomfortable saying them. 'And for your information, you're the last man on earth I'd sleep with!'

'And you're the last woman I'd sleep with,' Alex shot back, seething with irritation, 'which makes your claim that I fathered your child utterly ridiculous and totally without foundation. And having clarified that, I think it's time you made your way back to wherever you came from.'

'I n-never said you fathered my child,' she stammered, and he looked at her in growing exasperation. 'Daisy is my sister's child. You slept with my *sister*, Dr Westerling. Slept with her and then left her to deal with the consequences.'

Her *sister*?

There was another prolonged silence, broken only by the distant rush of waves hitting the beach and the occasional shriek of a seagull.

His first impulse was to ask whether her sister was blonde but he suppressed it and looked at her, carefully concealing his emotions.

'And where is your sister now?'

'She's dead.'

Alex saw the anguish in her dark eyes before she quickly veiled it. Suddenly the baby started to cry miserably, almost as if it had understood that something dreadful had happened.

Reluctantly accepting that this wasn't a problem that was going to go away in anything like a hurry, he jerked his head towards the cottage.

'You'd better come inside.'

Vowing that from now on he was going to lead a life of celibacy, Alex gritted his teeth, opened the front door and walked into his house.

There was a gasp of surprise behind him and the girl stopped dead, still clutching the sobbing child.

Alex flung his jacket onto the nearest sofa and glanced at her impatiently. 'What?'

'It's just— I didn't…' She looked around her, unable to disguise her surprise. 'I thought you lived in a cottage.'

'It is a cottage. Well, actually it's four cottages knocked into one.'

She gazed around her. 'It's…not what I expected…'

Alex looked at her with undisguised irritation and then transferred his gaze to the baby, who was still howling. 'Can you do something about the noise? Does it need changing or something?'

She dragged her eyes away from the enormous speakers set in each corner of the spacious living room and glared at him disapprovingly. 'The baby is not an "*it*", Dr Westerling,' she said stiffly, bouncing the baby on her hip in an attempt to soothe her. 'She's a little girl and her name is Daisy. She's your daughter.'

'So you keep telling me.' Alex gritted his teeth as he loosened his tie. He wasn't going to argue with her while there was so much noise in the background. 'For crying out loud, give her to me.' Without waiting for her reply, he reached out and took the child, lifting her onto his shoulder with calm confidence and placing a large hand on the centre of her back. Without looking at the girl, he walked over towards the huge glass windows that stretched across his enormous living room and looked out over the sea. Normally the view soothed him but with the baby howling in his ear his head was starting to pound.

'She might be hungry…' the girl offered tentatively, and he shot her an impatient look.

'So feed her. Presumably you've brought some food on your little trip?'

She nodded. 'I'll need to go back to the car and get my bags.'

Get her bags?

What bags?

He watched her vanish back up the path towards the little red car that he only now spotted at the top of his drive. How could he have missed seeing it when he'd driven home? He closed his eyes briefly and felt an overwhelming urge to sleep. It was hardly surprising he hadn't seen her car. He was so tired he would have driven past a herd of elephants without giving them a second glance.

It suddenly occurred to him that the terrible noise had stopped and the baby was now staring fixedly at his face.

He stared back, looking for something familiar, some part of himself that might suggest that this was indeed his child.

She had blue eyes, that was true enough, but, then, so did plenty of children so that didn't mean anything and she didn't seem to have much in the way of hair at all so he couldn't use that as a pointer.

Without warning her mouth spread into a gorgeous smile and he found himself smiling back.

'So you think you can charm me, do you, blue eyes?' he murmured softly, lifting a finger and rubbing her cheek gently. 'I probably ought to warn you that I grew out of being taken in by a female smile a long time ago. I'm immune.'

She cooed happily and he carried on talking quietly to

her until he heard footsteps and turned to find the girl standing in his doorway carrying several large bags.

His smile faded. 'Presumably you'll find the food eventually?'

She flushed and rummaged in one of the bags, pulling out a cool bag, bibs and several small pots. 'Where's your kitchen?'

He lifted an eyebrow. 'You want a tour of my house?'

She bit her lip. 'No, I do not want a tour of your house, but unless you want carrot purée on those pristine white sofas, Dr Westerling, I suggest we feed her in the kitchen.'

The baby gurgled happily and sucked her fists and Alex accepted the inevitable.

'We feed her,' he said through gritted teeth, 'and then we talk. Leave those bags by the door. It will stop you having to carry them so far when you want to take them back to the car.'

'I won't be going back to the car, but I refuse to argue this with you in front of D-Daisy,' she stammered, following him across the gleaming wooden floor towards the kitchen. 'Babies are like barometers. She's picking up the atmosphere.'

'Then she's a bright girl.' Alex stalked into his state-of-the-art kitchen and waved an arm. 'Help yourself. What do you need?'

'Hot water and access to a microwave to heat her food?'

Alex extended a lean brown hand. 'Give me the jar—I'll do the heating.'

'It isn't a jar. I make all her food myself.' The girl handed him a plastic pot and he scraped the mushy contents into a bowl and stuck it in the microwave with an expression of distaste.

'That looks utterly revolting.'

'It's nutritious and she loves it.'

Alex didn't argue. Instead he reached into a cupboard and pulled out a high chair, ignoring her look of amazement.

'I have nieces and nephews,' he said shortly, wondering why he was proffering an explanation, 'but as you seem to think you know everything about me, you probably already know that.'

'How old are they?'

'That's none of your business. I never discuss my family with strangers, and you,' he said icily, 'are most definitely a stranger.'

She flushed slightly and settled the baby on her lap.

He noticed that she was avoiding looking him in the eye and took that as another sign of her guilty conscience.

She had to be lying.

She *had* to be lying, otherwise…

Tensing his jaw, he removed the food from the microwave and put it on the table, but the girl's eyes were fixed on Daisy as she gave her a bottle.

'I have to give her some milk first or she's just too hungry to concentrate on the food,' she murmured, and Alex rolled his eyes.

'Spare me the detail.'

'You're going to need the detail, Dr Westerling. I'm no longer able to take sole responsibility for your child. I need help.'

Still not looking at him, she smiled down at the child who sucked greedily at the bottle of milk.

The smile completely altered her appearance and Alex found his attention caught. She had delicate, almost elfin features, her dark eyes fringed with long, even darker lashes that made her cheeks seem even paler. Her dark hair was pulled back from her face and fastened in a ponytail and she didn't appear to be wearing a scrap of make-up.

He stared at her, fascinated. He wasn't used to women who didn't wear make-up.

All the women he knew wore make-up. Even the ones

that favoured the 'natural' look spent at least half an hour
in front of the mirror before they emerged from the bathroom.

Not this girl, it seemed.

Despite the fact that it was August and the weather was
hot, she was wearing a blouse that buttoned up to her neck
and a skirt that buttoned down to her ankles. She looked
at him periodically, reproach and a certain wariness evident
in her huge eyes. She looked fresh and innocent and very,
very young.

Evidently she was expecting him to drag her off to his
lair and have his evil way with her, he reflected wryly. She
obviously thoroughly disapproved of him and her blatant
condemnation made him vaguely irritated and more than a
little uncomfortable.

She reminded him of Little Red Riding Hood and she
was making him feel like a very, *very* bad wolf.

Assuring himself that she probably wasn't innocent at
all, he turned away and cursed softly under his breath.

He had more sense than to be taken in by a pair of wide
eyes and an innocent expression. The girl was trouble. It
was more than likely that she knew full well that the baby
wasn't his but had identified him as an unlimited source of
cash.

Thanks to all the press coverage, he was a constant target
for women seeking an easy way to supplement their income
and this girl was no exception. Despite that innocent expression, she was trying to fleece him.

He paced the kitchen while she finished feeding the baby,
his temper held on a very tight leash.

Finally the baby was fed and looked decidedly sleepy.

The girl glanced at her watch. 'It's six o'clock. She usually has her bath and goes straight to bed. Do you have a
travel cot?'

'Yes, but be warned that she's only going into it on a
temporary basis while we discuss what needs to be dis-

cussed,' Alex bit out. 'Once we're finished, you're both going home.'

'She no longer has a mother,' the girl said, her voice decidedly wobbly as she scooped the baby out of the high chair. 'It isn't fair to deny her a father as well. As far as I'm concerned, her home is with you until we work out what to do.'

Alex closed his eyes and cursed all women under his breath and then strode out of the kitchen and up the staircase that led to the bedrooms, aware that she was struggling to keep up with his pace.

He flung open a door that led off the long landing and she gasped in delight.

'What a perfect room!'

Alex gave her a frosty look. 'Well, don't get too used to it. She's only going to be in it for an hour.'

'No, she isn't.' The girl placed the child on the floor and reached for the bag that she'd carried upstairs. 'I need to get her changed. I'll join you downstairs when I've finished.'

Totally unused to being ordered around by anyone, especially in his own home, Alex found himself lost for words and retreated downstairs and poured himself a large whisky.

Jenny took a final look at the sleeping baby, delaying the final moment when she was going to have to face Alex.

She had to admit that she found him monumentally intimidating. He was physically powerful, of course, but it wasn't just that. There was something about him. An air of self-belief that had probably been passed down through generations of Westerlings.

She'd expected him to be shocked by her announcement that Daisy was his baby but he'd barely flickered an eyelid. She wondered what it would take to disturb that legendary cool. Remembering his caustic comments, she shivered slightly.

He was everything she'd expected. Staggeringly good-looking, arrogant and loaded with self-confidence. And he was obviously going to take some persuading that Daisy was his.

She reached the bottom of the stairs and paused. He'd opened the French windows and was standing on the wooden deck outside, staring over the sand dunes towards the sea.

Taking a deep breath, she walked towards him, her nails digging into her palms.

He must have heard her because he turned instantly, a glass in his hand, his startling blue eyes cool and discouraging.

He'd discarded the tie and unbuttoned the first few buttons of his shirt. With his tousled hair and the rough stubble grazing his hard jaw, he looked dangerous and thoroughly disreputable and absolutely nothing like a doctor.

She wondered if he shaved before he saw patients.

'Is she asleep?'

Jenny nodded. 'Yes. I've left the door open so that we can hear her if she wakes.'

'Fine. Let's talk. Fast. I want to get on with my evening.'

Jenny took several deep breaths. He certainly wasn't making things easy for her but then what had she expected? That he'd accept Daisy with open arms? Of course not!

He gave a sigh and ran a hand over his face, as if trying to keep himself awake. She suddenly recalled his comment about having been up for thirty-six hours and her mouth tightened. Obviously he'd been living up to his reputation for partying.

He suppressed a yawn. 'Perhaps you'd better start by telling me who your sister was.'

'Her name was Chloe.' She almost choked as she said her sister's name. 'Chloe Phillips.'

He didn't hesitate. 'I've never met anyone by that name.'

His instant dismissal intensified the lump to her throat. How could he have forgotten Chloe so quickly? Obviously everything she'd heard about him had been correct. That he moved from one woman to another without forming any sort of attachment.

She chewed her lip. 'I wouldn't really expect someone with your reputation to remember one particular night. You've dated so many women it must be impossible to keep track.'

There was a brief pause and then he threw back his head and laughed. 'You really disapprove of me, don't you?'

She hid her surprise. She'd expected him to be angry or embarrassed by her accusations, instead of which he seemed amused. Not by the merest flicker of an eyelid did he indicate that her damning words had had any impact on him whatsoever. Evidently his dreadful reputation didn't worry him in the slightest.

He looked at her keenly. 'How did your sister die?'

His tone was surprisingly gentle and Jenny swallowed hard. 'She had a pulmonary embolus after the birth. It was all very sudden. I—I didn't even know she was having the baby,' she choked, unable to continue, and suddenly she felt his hand on her shoulder, pushing her towards one of the wooden chairs that faced out towards the sea.

'Sit down,' he said roughly. 'I'll get you a drink.'

Jenny struggled to contain the tears, furious with herself. She'd cried so many tears over Chloe she didn't think she had any left inside her. And she really, really didn't want to cry in front of Alex Westerling. He was the last person she'd turn to for sympathy.

He was partly to blame for the whole sorry situation.

He pressed a glass into her hands and she sipped the fiery liquid, choking slightly as it hit the back of her throat.

'Ugh! That's disgusting.'

'It's single malt,' he said dryly, a hint of amusement in his blue eyes. 'Certainly not disgusting.'

She screwed up her face but forced herself to take another tentative sip. 'I'm OK now.' She lifted her chin. 'Sorry. It's just that I still can't quite believe she's…' She broke off and swallowed hard. 'She was younger than me, you see.'

His eyes narrowed. 'Younger?'

'She was twenty when she had Daisy. She died a few days later.'

Alex pulled out the chair next to her. 'Look—I'm sorry about your sister and I can see she's left you with a hell of a problem, but—'

'Daisy isn't a *problem*, Dr Westerling,' Jenny said passionately, her hand shaking so much that some of the contents of the glass sloshed onto her fingers. 'Daisy is wonderful and without her I don't know what I'd—'

'All right, calm down.' Alex reached out and took the glass from her. 'I'll have that before you spill any more.' He put the glass on the table and sighed. 'I'm sorry. That wasn't the most tactful thing to say but I'm decidedly short on sleep and saying the right thing is hard when you're as knackered as I am.'

She looked at him, startled by the apology. She hadn't thought he'd be the sort of man who would apologise easily.

'Perhaps if you spent less time socialising you wouldn't be so tired.'

The moment the words left her mouth she bit her lip, wishing she could retract them. 'I apologise,' she mumbled, her cheeks growing red. 'That was very rude of me.'

Alex laughed. 'You were quite happy to turn up on my doorstep flinging wild accusations—why are you apologising for being rude?'

'They're not w-wild accusations,' Jenny stammered, her

cheeks still pink, 'and just because we have a problem it doesn't give me the excuse to forget my manners.'

Alex gave a wry smile. 'I think we've moved slightly beyond manners, don't you? And now you need to listen to me.' His smile faded and voice was firm. 'I don't remember your sister, but I do know that I don't sleep with children and your sister appears to have fallen into that category. I don't know what she told you, but there's no way I can be the father of her baby.'

'She spent the night with you.'

His increased tension was barely perceptible. 'Do you have proof?'

Jenny nodded and reached for her bag, her hands shaking slightly. 'You were at the same party and she was…' She hesitated slightly, and then cleared her throat. 'She was drunk. You took her home.'

She dragged out an envelope and handed it to him.

Blue eyes locked onto hers for a long moment and then he dropped his gaze to the envelope and reached inside for the contents.

He flicked through them silently, a slight frown touching his brows. 'These pictures—'

'Were taken by one of the magazines. But they clearly show you dancing with her. "Alex Westerling dancing with a friend", the caption says—well, your *friend* was my sister. Chloe. So you see, Dr Westerling, you *did* know her.'

He paused to read the letter and leafed through the remaining photos, his handsome face inscrutable.

She decided that he was a very difficult man to read. He seemed to possess enviable control over his reactions.

'I may have danced with her, but she didn't spend the night in my flat.'

'She said she did.'

He yawned. 'Then she was lying.' He tossed the envelope onto the table and shook his head. 'Is that it?'

It? How could he be so maddeningly cool about the whole situation?

Jenny bit her lip. 'She came home very upset after that night. She didn't want to talk about it, but when the photographs were published the following week she eventually spilled the beans.'

Alex's eyes narrowed. 'And you didn't think that was odd?'

Jenny looked at him, uncomprehending. 'Why was it odd? She didn't want to tell me but when I saw the pictures it was obvious.'

'What was obvious?'

'That you'd had a relationship.'

'We were dancing,' Alex said mildly. 'That hardly constitutes a relationship. I dance with a lot of women.'

'You sleep with a lot of women, too,' she said, totally unthinkingly, and then gasped as she realised what she'd said.

Alex laughed. 'You seem to have studied my lifestyle in minute detail,' he drawled, his deep tones thoroughly masculine and more than a little disturbing. 'Why are you so interested in me, I wonder?'

Her heart suddenly beat faster. 'I'm not interested in you, Dr Westerling. Except when your thoughtless lifestyle affects my family. And you're not going to get away with it. Don't think you can walk away from your responsibilities this time.'

His blue eyes were suddenly cold. 'I have never walked away from my responsibilities, but I did not sleep with your sister,' he said curtly, 'and a simple DNA test should prove that to everyone's satisfaction.'

Jenny looked at him in horror. 'No! I don't want anyone jabbing needles in Daisy unless it's absolutely essential.'

'If you're accusing me of being her father, then it's essential in my book,' Alex bit out, and Jenny shook her head.

'No. I already know you're her father. I don't need proof.'

'Well, I'm afraid I do.' Alex rose to his feet in a fluid movement. 'And I intend to sort this out as quickly as possible.'

'How?'

'If you won't agree to a blood test, I'll contact my lawyers first thing tomorrow.' Alex suppressed another yawn. 'Once they've proved beyond a shadow of a doubt that I didn't spend the night with your sister, you can look elsewhere for the financial support you're obviously seeking.'

Jenny stared at him helplessly.

He'd totally missed the point but, then, someone as rich as Alex Westerling was bound to think that everything in life revolved around money.

'I'm not seeking financial support,' she told him, her voice quiet. 'I'm not interested in your money. I just need help with Daisy and I want Daisy to know her father. She can't grow up not knowing either parent. It wouldn't be fair. She needs to know her daddy.'

Alex closed his eyes briefly. 'I'm not her "*daddy*". What's your name?'

Jenny stared at him. 'Pardon?'

'I asked you your name,' he said wearily. 'If we're going to have an argument it's usually helpful to know how to address each other.'

'Jenny.' Her voice wasn't quite as steady as she would have liked. 'Jenny Phillips.'

His slight smile affected her more than she cared to admit.

'Well, Jenny Phillips, you can take Daisy off to wherever you were planning on staying and as soon as I have a result from my lawyers I'll be in touch.'

Jenny didn't move. 'I'm planning on staying here.'

An ominous silence stretched between them. 'Say that again?'

She swallowed, wondering why she was finding this so hard. It had all seemed wonderfully simple when she'd planned it.

But then she hadn't met the real Alex Westerling and all the imaginings in the world hadn't prepared her for the reality.

'Daisy and I are staying with you, Dr Westerling. It makes sense. You can get to know her and help with her care.'

'Staying with me?' His blue eyes glittered dangerously and his voice was satiny smooth. 'Considering your outspoken views on my wicked reputation I'm surprised you're prepared to risk it, Miss Phillips. Surely there's a strong likelihood that you won't escape unscathed?'

His silky tone doubled her pulse rate but she forced herself not to react to his sarcasm. 'We both know your taste doesn't run to dark-haired women,' she replied, her voice remarkably steady considering the disrupted state of her emotions. 'And as I don't find you remotely attractive I'm fairly confident that I can restrain myself.'

It was a lie, of course. How could any woman not find him attractive? He was impossibly handsome and his total indifference to his startling good looks only intensified his appeal.

But she wasn't interested in a man with no morals, no matter how good-looking he was.

And Alex Westerling had absolutely no morals.

There was a brief silence and then he threw back his head and laughed. 'Ouch. Well, that's put me in my place. All right, stay if you dare. Frankly I'm too tired to argue with you. But what are you going to do when I prove that she isn't my child?'

Seeing the masculine challenge in his eyes Jenny's heart beat slightly faster but she lifted her chin, determined not to show him how uncomfortable he made her feel. 'That isn't going to happen, Dr Westerling.'

'That is exactly what is going to happen, *Miss Phillips*,' Alex returned smoothly, mimicking her formality, 'but if you really want to risk living with me, that's up to you. I'm going to bed and frankly I don't give a damn where you sleep as long as you and that baby don't wake me up.'

And with that he drained his glass, thumped it down on the table and strode away from her.

CHAPTER THREE

ALEX awoke to the smell of freshly baked rolls and strong coffee.

Remembering the events of the night before, he gave a groan of disbelief and covered his eyes with a forearm, trying to block out reality.

People had always warned him that his sins would come back to haunt him and it turned out that they were right.

At this moment there was a bundle of trouble waiting for him downstairs in his kitchen.

A baby who he was fairly sure wasn't his, complete with doting aunt who obviously thought he was a wicked seducer of innocent females.

He glanced at the clock and realised that it was almost seven o'clock. Which meant that he was expected at work in an hour.

Promising himself a really long lie-in at the weekend, he forced himself out of bed and into the shower before making the phone call that needed to be made.

By the time he appeared downstairs he was feeling better. His lawyer had been suitably reassuring and he was confident that the situation would be resolved quickly.

All in all he was feeling back in control and he was totally unprepared for the scene of domesticity in his usually pristine, undisturbed designer kitchen.

In the five years he'd lived in the house, he'd never invited a woman back to his home. This was his territory.

A totally bachelor environment.

But not any more.

Soft rolls, baked to a light brown, lay neatly on a rack,

cooling, and a pot of steaming coffee sat in the middle of the table.

The baby was strapped in the high chair, happily gnawing on a piece of roll while Jenny chatted to her and spooned cereal into her mouth. She broke off and blushed when she saw Alex.

It occurred to him that she blushed more than any female he'd ever met.

'Oh— Good morning. We made breakfast— I hope you don't mind.'

If he hadn't been so stunned he would have laughed. She'd invaded his house and here she was checking that he didn't mind that she'd used the facilities? She was like a child at a party, desperate to be on her very best behaviour.

'You're obviously not a very experienced squatter,' he observed dryly. 'You're not supposed to apologise for making yourself at home.'

'I'm not a squatter.' She lifted her small chin and her tone was incredibly dignified. 'But I know I'm not your guest either. I'm aware that I'm here under sufferance.'

'You're here because frankly I was too knackered to throw you out last night,' Alex told her bluntly, eyeing the rolls and wondering why he suddenly felt like eating breakfast. He never ate breakfast. 'You made them this morning?'

Jenny nodded. 'Daisy woke early. She often does. We didn't want to wake you up so we came downstairs. Help yourself.'

'I don't eat breakfast.' The warm, freshly baked smell teased his nostrils and he gritted his teeth.

'Breakfast is the most important meal of the day,' she said, looking at him calmly. 'You ought to eat.'

'When I want your advice on my eating habits, I'll ask for it,' he growled, forcing himself to ignore the delicious smell and focus on the issues in hand. 'I've just spoken to my lawyer.'

She stiffened, the spoon poised in mid-air. 'Do lawyers always start work this early?'

'If you pay them enough,' Alex observed dryly, reaching for a mug and pouring himself some coffee. 'He's confident that he can find out who your sister was with that night.'

Jenny put the spoon to Daisy's lips. 'She was with you.'

'So you keep saying. I disagree.' He took a sip of coffee and almost groaned with pleasure. It was delicious. He hadn't known that he possessed coffee this good. Where the hell had she found it?

'Dr Westerling…' She rested the spoon on the bowl and looked him in the eye. 'I know you slept with my sister so all this denial is pointless. I'm sure your lawyer will confirm the truth soon enough.'

'I'm banking on it,' he said softly. 'I just hope you don't learn something about your sister that you'd rather have not known.'

She tensed. 'What exactly is that supposed to mean?'

'Only that I'm almost totally sure I never slept with your sister—which means that someone else did.'

Her lips tightened and she picked the spoon up again. '"Almost totally sure". Which means you're not sure at all. Has anyone ever told you that your morals are extremely questionable?'

'I'm thirty-four years of age and my morals are nobody's business but my own,' Alex said, wondering why her words irritated him so much. Usually he was totally indifferent to people's opinion of him. 'I'm as sure as I can be that I never had any sort of relationship with your sister, but it was fifteen months ago!'

She regarded him steadily. 'And you have absolutely no idea who you were sleeping with fifteen months ago, have you? You need to employ someone to find out.'

Her quiet tone was loaded with accusation and Alex ran a hand over the back of his neck, feeling more uncomfortable than he cared to admit. The truth was that she was right. In a way. He *didn't* know exactly who he'd been with fifteen months ago and he didn't need her to remind him that his track record for long-term relationships was appalling.

It wasn't something he cared to dwell on.

'Did your sister actually tell you I was the father?'

'Yes.' She stirred the food slightly to cool it down.

Alex gritted his teeth, wondering whether she always believed everything she was told without question. He was as sure as he could be that the baby wasn't his but only time would prove it.

In the meantime he had a job to do.

'I have to leave for work.' He drained his mug and deposited it on the table. 'You can stay here today.'

And hopefully by the end of the day his lawyer would have resolved the issue and he could boot her out.

She looked at him in that calm, unflustered way that he was beginning to recognise as a prelude to one of her cutting remarks about his disreputable behaviour.

He braced himself.

'If you're hoping to hide us away, Dr Westerling, you're going to be seriously disappointed.' Jenny undid the bib, wiped Daisy's mouth carefully and lifted her out of the high chair. 'We're coming with you. I'm starting work today. I've got a job in your department and Daisy has a place in the crèche.'

Alex stared at her, feeling outmanoeuvred for the first time in his life.

She had a job in his department?

'What the hell are you talking about? What job?'

'I'm a nurse, Dr Westerling,' she told him, cuddling Daisy with one hand while she cleared up with brisk efficiency. 'I've been working in A and E for two years, ever since I qualified, but I had to take a break when Chloe died. But I need to work now. We need the money. I've used up all my savings.'

Alex wasn't interested in her savings. He was struggling with the news that not only was she planning to be under his feet at home but that she was going to be working with him, too.

'How did you find out where I worked?'

'It wasn't hard. Every detail of your life is spread over the gossip columns.' She picked up a cloth and within minutes his kitchen was totally spotless. 'I wanted us to be a family so it was important that we worked in the same hospital if possible. I was delighted when they offered me a job in your department.'

She wanted them to be a family?

Alex opened his mouth and closed it again.

He couldn't even contemplate retribution because neither the nursing staff nor Personnel would have had the slightest clue as to the problem they were introducing into his usually well-ordered bachelor lifestyle by employing Jenny Phillips.

Finally he found his voice. 'Look, I'm sorry about your sister but we need to get a few things straight,' he growled, 'We are not "a family". We will never be "a family". You can stay here for just as long as it takes my lawyer to prove that I'm not the baby's father, and then you're on your own.'

She appeared totally unmoved by his threats. 'And if he proves that you are Daisy's father?'

Alex tensed. He refused to even contemplate that possibility.

'Then we'll deal with it,' he said abruptly. 'But for now you're nothing more to me than a lodger. And a very unwelcome one at that.'

'It's absolute heaven to have more staff,' Tina told Jenny as she showed her around. 'We were so busy yesterday that one of our consultants worked thirty-six hours on the trot with only a quick nap at his desk.'

'I've been up for thirty-six hours.'

Jenny's eyes widened. 'Was that Alex Westerling?'

'You know him?'

Jenny shook her head quickly. 'Well, no, not exactly, but—'

'Don't tell me,' Tina said dryly, 'you've read about him in the newspapers. He's not very good at keeping a low profile is our Alex. Well, I'd better warn you that you don't want to believe everything you read. Whatever he gets up to in his spare time, Alex is a fantastic doctor.'

Jenny hid her surprise. Was he? She had to admit that she hadn't given any thought to his abilities as a doctor. In fact, she couldn't even imagine Alex as a doctor. When she looked at him all she saw was the man. If she'd had to chose a suitable career for him it would have been pirate or highwayman!

She closed her eyes and pushed the thought away, dealing with the sudden awareness that it had been overwork that had contributed to the tiredness she'd seen in his eyes the previous night.

The knowledge made her feel surprisingly uncomfortable.

When he'd mentioned that he'd been awake all night she'd assumed that he was living up to his reputation for wild partying.

She'd just assumed that medicine must be low on his list of priorities.

Tina was still chatting. 'He makes sure the department runs as smoothly as possibly even when we're desperate for staff. And, of course, August is always difficult because we have an influx of new doctors who don't know the ropes.'

Jenny nodded, trying to change the subject. 'So where do you want me this morning?'

'I thought we'd throw you straight in the deep end.' Tina smiled. 'You can work in the main area with me.'

She'd barely finished her sentence when a phone rang.

'That's the ambulance hotline,' Tina told her, hurrying to answer it. 'More trouble on the way, no doubt.'

Jenny listened to the one-sided phone call, trying to pick up clues as to what was coming in to the department. All she could ascertain was that the patient was in considerable pain.

Tina replaced the phone. 'How are you on diving-related emergencies?'

Jenny shook her head apologetically. 'I worked in London. I've never seen one.'

'Then this is your lucky day,' the unit sister muttered, picking up the phone and dialling. 'Alex? You know you said that you wanted to be rescued from that meeting—' She broke off and listened for a second. 'Yeah, they're bringing in a diver—sounds like decompression. OK—see you in a mo.'

She replaced the receiver and hurried towards Resus, taking Jenny with her.

'Obviously, because we're by the coast, we get divers in here periodically. If they're very bad we transfer them to the diving medicine unit. Alex will decide.'

Jenny stiffened slightly. All she could think about was his careless treatment of her sister. 'What about the other doctors? Isn't there anyone else that can deal with it?'

'If they have to, they will, obviously.' Tina grabbed a pack from a shelf and placed it on a trolley in readiness. 'But this is Alex's field really. He's done some diving himself and he spent some time at the diving medicine unit so he knows what he's doing.'

As she finished speaking the doors swung open and the paramedics hurried through, accompanied by Alex.

'What's the story?'

The paramedics moved the patient across onto the trolley. 'This is Pete Warwick. He was on the beach this afternoon and collapsed complaining of numbness in his legs. His friends called us.'

Alex nodded and turned his attention to the patient. 'How are you feeling now, Pete?'

The man groaned slightly. 'Awful. Everything hurts.' He winced slightly. 'Mostly my shoulders and elbows.'

Alex looked at Jenny who was poised at the head of the trolley, nothing in his gaze revealing that she was anything other than another member of the emergency team. 'Give him high-flow oxygen and let's get a line in. I want to take some bloods.'

Jenny placed the mask over the patient's mouth and nose and adjusted the flow of oxygen carefully.

Alex was still examining the patient. 'Does the pain get worse if I move your arms?'

The man gasped and nodded, the pain visible in his face.

'There's no localised tenderness but there is some swelling and you've got a rash.' Alex ran a hand over his skin. 'When did you last dive?'

The man closed his eyes and Jenny moved the mask slightly so that he could answer. 'Yesterday. My legs feel numb now and my back hurts.'

'Did you do multiple dives?'

Pete hesitated and then nodded. 'Yeah. I know you're not supposed to but it was so great down there and I thought I'd be OK.'

Alex continued to talk to the man, questioning him about his method of computing bottom and ascent times, asking about stoppages and the conditions in the water, about the length of time between the dive and onset of symptoms.

It was all totally alien to Jenny. She'd worked in A and E for almost two years but she'd never seen a case like this one. Why did it matter whether the water had been cold or what the currents had been like? Obviously the questions carried some significance or presumably Alex wouldn't be asking them. She was fascinated and dying to know more, but she didn't like to question him while the patient was listening. Besides, they hadn't established any sort of professional relationship yet. She didn't feel comfortable asking questions.

She hadn't managed to separate Alex the doctor from Alex the wicked seducer.

And Alex was using standard resuscitation techniques, she assured herself, handing the venflon to the SHO who was trying to find a vein. There was nothing unfamiliar about the steps he was taking—just the reasons behind them.

'Once you've taken the blood get a unit of saline up,' Alex instructed as he continued his examination. 'Pete, you did too many dives and you came up too fast. You've got something called type one decompression sickness.'

Jenny listened in fascination and resolved to pluck up the courage to ask him about it later.

His gaze lifted and he looked straight at her. 'Get me the diving medical centre on the phone, please. I think we need to transfer him.'

Tina jerked her head towards the phone. 'The number's stuck on the wall.'

Jenny dialled and found herself talking to the duty diving doctor.

Alex strode over and relieved her of the phone. 'Chris? How are you doing? I've got a customer for you…' He quickly outlined the patient's condition and gave details of the dive and the history before listening to his colleague.

Finally he replaced the phone and strode back to his patient. 'We're transferring you to the diving medical centre,' he told him. 'Tina, can we give him some aspirin, please, and arrange for an ambulance?'

Considering the amount of pain the man seemed to be suffering, Jenny was surprised that Alex was giving Pete aspirin.

His gaze flickered to hers. 'Severe decompression can

cause capillary sludging,' he told her, obviously reading her mind, 'and it's the only analgesia I'm prepared to risk. Strong analgesia can mask recompression responses.'

Jenny nodded, grateful for his explanation, wishing that she'd been more knowledgeable for their first working encounter.

They prepared the man for the short transfer and in no time at all the ambulance crew arrived, ready to collect him.

Alex did a quick handover to the SHO who was going to accompany the patient and then went with the team to load him into the ambulance.

Jenny set about restocking Resus with Tina. 'I've never looked after anyone with decompression sickness before. I felt decidedly out of my depth,' she confessed, and then smiled as she realised what she'd said. 'Pardon the pun.'

Tina laughed. 'You did fine.'

'How come he only started getting symptoms today if it was yesterday that he was diving?'

Tina frowned. 'I don't know, actually. You'll have to ask Alex. He knows everything.'

As if on cue, Alex strolled back into the room. 'What do I know?'

'Jenny was asking why it took so long for the diver to show symptoms.'

Jenny coloured slightly. She would rather have not drawn attention to herself and she was still having trouble regarding him in a professional capacity.

Doctor, she reminded herself firmly, concentrating on the stethoscope looped casually round his neck. Today he was a doctor. Doctor. Doctor.

'Symptoms can occur from several minutes up to forty-eight hours after diving,' Alex explained, not by a flicker of an eyelid betraying the fact that they were at loggerheads. 'Decompression sickness is the result of gas bubbles travelling to various parts of the body.'

'And that's why he had pains in his joints?'

Alex nodded. 'It's known as "the bends".' He didn't follow his dive tables closely enough. He spent too long on the bottom and came up too fast. It could have been worse. He'll be OK once they've sorted him out at the dive centre.'

Tina smiled. 'In all the rush and panic, I didn't even have the chance to introduce you to our new staff nurse. This is Jenny. Jenny Phillips.'

Alex's blue gaze was decidedly cool as it flickered in her direction. 'We've met,' he said shortly, and turned on his heel and left the room without further conversation.

Tina stared after him, visibly shocked. 'What's got into him?'

Jenny ripped open a giving set and unravelled it ready so it could be attached to a bag of saline quickly if the next patient required it. She had absolutely no intention of confessing, but she knew exactly what had got to Alex Westerling.

Her.

Jenny enjoyed her first day more than she'd anticipated. It had helped that she'd been incredibly busy and that had prevented her from dwelling on her problems with Alex.

But she found working so closely with him distinctly unsettling as she tried to reconcile the doctor she saw in action with her preconceived views on the man.

Her head buzzed with conflicting signals.

She'd dismissed him as careless and shallow but as a doctor he was obviously extremely talented and well regarded.

The entire staff seemed to worship him.

How would they react if they knew what he was really like? she wondered as she collected a very contented but tired Daisy from the hospital crèche and drove out of town towards Alex's home. What would they say if they knew how badly he'd treated Chloe? They only saw the capable, self-assured doctor and obviously he behaved in a suitably

responsible fashion when he was at work. They didn't
know that he was a man with so few morals that he was
capable of leaving a young girl pregnant.

Her mouth tightened as she parked the car outside the
cottages and lifted the baby out of the car seat.

From his comments, it seemed as though he was going
to do everything possible to dodge his responsibilities towards Daisy.

In a way she was glad that he'd contacted his lawyer.
She had every confidence that he would produce concrete
evidence to show that Alex Westerling was Daisy's father.

And then surely he wouldn't refuse to be part of her
future?

Alex let himself into the house, dropped his bag on the
polished floor and threw his jacket over the nearest chair.

He was hot, tired and seething with irritation following
another fruitless discussion with hospital management over
staffing levels in the A and E department.

It was high summer, the place was flooded with tourists
and everyone was worked to the bone.

In theory he had the weekend off—the first one for a
month—but he was well aware that there was every likelihood that he'd be called in to help if things became too
stressful for the staff.

And if that happened he had every intention of calling
the chief executive of the hospital. If he had to forfeit his
precious weekend off then so could the hospital management.

Perhaps if the guy experienced the reality at first hand
he might be more sympathetic to requests for more staff.

Alex flexed his aching shoulders and looked out of the
huge windows across the sand. Normally the tension
leached out of him as soon as he reached his home, but not
any more.

His home had suddenly become a source of tension too.

He'd passed Jenny's car on the way in so he knew she was here.

With the baby.

The baby that wasn't his.

Any hope he'd had that his lawyer would have been able to clear the matter up quickly had been dispelled by a quick conversation before he'd left the hospital. It seemed that it was going to take some time and the help of a private investigator to produce the evidence that Alex required.

Which meant that for the time being he was stuck with them. Unless he threw them out.

His head was suddenly filled with the disturbing memory of the baby smiling up at him and Jenny's eyes filling as she'd told him about Chloe.

He gritted his teeth and knew that he couldn't throw them out. Not until he'd been given some answers.

Cursing himself for being a soft touch, he decided that what he needed was exercise. Something to take his mind off the frustrations of the day.

He could run or he could swim.

The sea sparkled temptingly and he opted for the swim. Although it was early evening it was still surprisingly warm and hopefully the cool water would clear his head.

He took the stairs two at a time and then paused when he heard laughter coming from one of his bathrooms.

He'd given her a key so that she could let herself in, only too aware that if he hadn't she would have been more than capable of forcing a confrontation in A and E in front of his colleagues, and that was something he was keen to avoid.

For the time being he didn't want anyone knowing she was staying with him.

Hearing more laughter, he pushed open the bathroom door and stood still, his attention caught by the antics of the little girl.

She was chuckling with delight as she splashed herself, totally confident and happy in the water.

Jenny was completely soaked and Alex's eyes flickered downwards, his gaze drawn to the swell of her small breasts under the damp, clinging material.

Unaware of his presence, Jenny leaned forward to kiss the baby.

'Ow!' She winced as Daisy locked a fist in her hair and tugged at her ponytail. 'Now look what you've done, you minx.'

Her dark hair tumbled loose around her shoulders but she ignored it and scooped the baby out of the bath and laid her carefully on the towel that she had ready.

Alex watched, curiously. Whatever the circumstances of the baby's conception there was absolutely no doubt that Jenny adored her niece.

'There—was that nice, angel?' She dried the baby carefully and then reached for a nappy and noticed Alex. Her smile vanished and she looked at him warily, self-consciously adjusting her T-shirt. 'Oh. Hello. We didn't hear you.'

'Evidently.'

With her soft dark hair around her shoulders and no bra she looked completely different from the disapproving young woman he'd met at breakfast or the professional nurse he'd worked with all day.

She looked…

She looked…

Damn! What the hell was the matter with him? This woman had come into his life for the express purpose of causing trouble and here he was lounging in the doorway noticing all sorts of things he shouldn't be noticing.

He definitely needed to plunge himself into cold water.

'I'm going for a swim,' he said shortly, and she looked surprised.

'Oh. But you've only just come in.'

He ground his teeth. This was why he'd never lived with a woman. They expected an explanation for everything.

'And I'm immediately going out.'

'Right.' She brushed her hair out of her eyes. 'It's just that I thought you might want to spend some time with Daisy before she goes to sleep.'

'Well, you thought wrong.'

Daisy chose that particular moment to chuckle and smile at him and the muscles in his shoulders tensed even more.

He didn't need this.

'Look…' His tone was harsh. 'I don't do family stuff, OK? I never have and the sooner you realise that the better for both of us. I live on my own and that's the way I like it. If I want to swim in the sea, I swim. I don't answer to anyone and I have absolutely no wish to cuddle a child who isn't mine.'

Her gaze was steady. 'But she *is* yours, Dr Westerling. You may not be able to remember the names of your girl-friends but my sister was different. She wouldn't have— well, she didn't have lots of partners.' She blushed slightly. 'If she said you were the father then that's good enough for me.'

'It isn't good enough for *me*. This is England. I'm in-nocent until proven guilty and, for goodness' sake, stop calling me Dr Westerling. If you're intent on living in my house and ruining my life, you might as well use my first name,' he said irritably, casting an impatient look in her direction before striding off towards his bedroom to collect what he needed for his swim.

Jenny dressed Daisy and sat her on the floor.

'Your daddy behaves like a little boy,' she said wearily. 'Everything seems to revolve around him with no thought for others. He comes from a very rich family, you know. He was probably brought up by a series of nannies and doesn't really know what family life is. We're going to have to show him.'

Daisy cooed and sucked her fists and Jenny stuffed some supplies into a bag and lifted the baby onto her shoulder.

'We're going to start by hiding that whisky bottle and making him eat breakfast. How do you fancy having your supper on the beach? We can watch him swim.'

She was absolutely determined that Alex wasn't going to avoid them.

Daisy was his child and the sooner he started accepting her as part of his life, the better.

She carried Daisy to the kitchen, prepared her bottle and then walked out onto the sand, carefully locking the doors behind her.

There were a few other people on the beach and she narrowed her eyes and squinted into the distance, trying to identify Alex.

She made out a lone swimmer moving smoothly through the waves and decided that it must be him.

Finding a towel and some shoes abandoned at a safe distance from the water's edge, she decided that they must belong to Alex.

'We'll just settle ourselves here and wait for him,' she said to Daisy, dropping the rug that she'd found in one of the cupboards and settling herself comfortably. She just wished that she could relax herself but the tension was really starting to get to her. Her heart was thumping and she felt incredibly nervous.

You didn't need to be a genius to know that he was going to be annoyed to see her there.

But what else was she supposed to do?

If he was going to continue to ignore Daisy, then it was up to her to try and bring the two of them together.

'You deserve to know your father, angel,' she muttered, settling Daisy on her lap and offering her the bottle.

The baby sucked greedily and while she fed Jenny stared

out to sea at the swimmer, watching the steady lift and fall of his arms as he cut through the water. Whoever it was, he was a powerful swimmer and she just knew it had to be Alex.

She sat on the blanket and fed the baby, totally unable to relax, knowing that the moment he saw her there'd be trouble.

When he finally emerged from the sea she tensed, preparing herself for the inevitable confrontation.

But as he moved closer all thoughts of confrontation vanished from her mind.

He was wearing the briefest pair of trunks she'd ever seen. They seemed to accentuate the muscular perfection of his powerful body and suddenly Jenny found she couldn't breathe.

She averted her eyes quickly, looking at the sea, the beach, anywhere as long as it wasn't at him.

But it was too late.

Just one glimpse had been enough. With the accuracy of a camera, her eyes had recorded the vision of Alex and stored it with appalling clarity in her befuddled brain.

'Are you stalking me?' He reached down and picked up his towel, his dark lashes clumped together, drips of water glistening on his hard cheekbones.

'No.' She sat stiffly, desperately trying not to look at him. 'But I won't let you avoid Daisy. She's part of your life, whether you like it or not.'

'Not,' he said grimly, rubbing the towel over his face and hair and draping it around his broad shoulders, 'as my lawyer will shortly prove. I thought I already made clear to you that I value my independence. I don't like being followed.'

He was drying his shoulders now and against her will her eyes followed the contour of his muscles, tracing the perfect curvature which indicated the degree of physical demands that he placed upon himself.

...ke so many of the doctors she met, Alex Westerling ... the body of an athlete, a physique that undoubtedly would have been the envy of most men.

Jenny looked away quickly, horrified by the direction of her thoughts.

Why did she care what sort of body he had?

She didn't want to notice his physique. She didn't care about his physique. She wasn't that shallow.

Looks didn't matter.

There were other things far more important, such as behaving in an honourable way, something which Alex evidently knew very little about.

Her slim shoulders sagged slightly.

Maybe this whole idea had been a mistake.

It was all very well to want Daisy to know her father, but what if her father wasn't worth knowing? What if he was the sort of man who never faced up to his responsibilities?

She was about to speak when she heard a shrill scream from further down the beach.

Alex stopped drying himself and stared in the direction of the sound. 'What…?'

A woman was running in their direction, carrying a little girl who was screaming loudly. 'Help me!'

Alex dropped the towel and sprinted towards her while Jenny stooped to pick up the rug and Daisy before hurrying to catch him up.

'What happened?'

'She trod on a jellyfish—there's a bit still stuck to her foot.' The mother started to sob hysterically and Alex's gaze flickered to Jenny, his message clear.

The mother was making the situation a thousand times worse.

Jenny immediately took the woman's arm. 'Try not to panic. Most of the jellyfish in these waters are relatively harmless.' She flung her rug on the ground and sat Daisy down, thankful that she was still too young to move about. 'Let me hold your daughter so that Dr Westerling can take a proper look at her.'

The woman relinquished her grip on the child without protest. 'You're a doctor?' She was looking at Alex as though he were an oasis in a desert. 'Oh, thank goodness. I was so worried—we're such a long way from civilisation and you read such dreadful things.'

They were on a Cornish beach— Hardly that far from civilisation!

Thinking that the woman was overreacting, Jenny glanced at Alex, expecting him to make a caustic comment, but he didn't. Instead, he bent down to examine the child's foot.

'It's swollen and it's obviously going to be causing her pain,' he said finally, glancing around him with a frown. 'We need some sea water.'

'We've left buckets and spades over there.' the woman gestured vaguely across the beach. 'But I don't want to leave her.'

Alex smiled, his blue eyes reassuring. 'She'll be fine with us and I need that sea water. Would you mind?'

Staring into his handsome face, the woman suddenly stopped crying and gave a self-conscious smile. 'I— If that's what you want, I'll go and fetch the bucket.'

'That's great,' Alex said smoothly, and Jenny resisted the temptation to roll her eyes.

What was it about her sex that made them behave like such idiots in the presence of a good-looking man?

She watched while the woman hurried away across the sand and then realised that Alex had turned his attention back to the little girl who was still crying quietly.

'What's your name, sweetheart?'

The little girl gulped. 'Amy. Are you really a doctor?'

Alex grinned. 'I'm really a doctor, Amy. Don't I look like a doctor?'

The girl stopped crying and her eyes were suddenly huge. 'You don't wear clothes and most doctors wear clothes. My doctor at home wears a tie.'

Alex laughed. 'I wear clothes when I'm at work, but at the moment I'm not working. I'm wearing my beach clothes. Just like you. And ties look silly with swimming trunks, don't you agree?'

Amy giggled but Jenny felt her face heat at yet another reminder of his decidedly disturbing state of undress.

Alex seemed supremely indifferent to the fact that he was wearing virtually nothing.

'Well, Amy…' he treated the little girl to another one of those smiles that seemed to knock women sideways '…as soon as your mummy comes back, we're going to rinse this foot of yours.' He glanced at Jenny. 'We need some vinegar.'

'I'll go and get some from the house,' she said immediately, and then hesitated and looked at Daisy.

Alex intercepted her glance. 'I'll keep an eye on her. But don't read anything into it.'

She ran back to the house, flinging open cupboards in the kitchen until she found the vinegar.

On impulse she sprinted up the stairs, pushed open the door to Alex's bedroom and grabbed a shirt that she saw lying on the bed.

She returned to find Alex bathing the foot in sea water while the mother stared at him in ill-concealed admiration

Gritting her teeth, Jenny thrust the shirt in his direction 'I thought you might like to put this on.'

'Thank you.' He took the shirt without further comment but something gleamed in his blue eyes and she coloured slightly.

Bother.

She hoped he didn't realised that seeing him naked was making her uncomfortable.

Satisfied that there were no more tentacles stuck to the

little foot, Alex reached for the vinegar. 'This should help,' he said. 'Do you have paracetamol syrup at home?'

'We're on holiday,' the woman said, looking at him meaningfully. 'We're staying at the Cliffside Hotel.'

Alex calmly ignored the blatant invitation. 'That's near a chemist so you should be able to pick some up. They stay open late at this time of year.'

Finally he was satisfied and he dressed the foot and lifted the little girl into his arms.

'Better now?'

She nodded. 'It still hurts a bit.'

He nodded sympathetically. 'It should feel better soon.' He handed her back to her mother with a smile. 'Any worries, take her up to A and E, but I don't think you'll have any problems. And next time you need to watch where you're stepping, young lady.'

The child nodded and stuck her thumb in her mouth. The mother cast a last longing look at Alex before picking up the bucket and struggling back along the beach towards the rest of their things.

Alex watched them go and Jenny wondered whether he even realised that he was still half-naked. It seemed not. Didn't he know the effect he had on people? All right, so he'd dragged the shirt on, but he hadn't bothered doing it up and she kept catching thoroughly disturbing glimpses of a muscular chest covered in curling dark hair. Against her will her eyes traced the line of dark hair down to where it disappeared into his swimming trunks and she felt her mouth dry.

'Well, that added a bit of excitement to my evening swim,' he said casually, stifling a yawn and reaching for the towel that he'd tossed on the rug.

'I'm surprised you didn't take up her invitation,' Jenny muttered, and he gave a cool smile.

'Maybe I will,' he drawled carelessly, but she suspected that he was just baiting her and watched silently as he draped the towel round his neck and ran his fingers through his damp hair to straighten it.

Suddenly aware that from her position on the rug her eyes were level with his powerful thighs, Jenny scrambled to her feet, her face flushed. All of a sudden all she could think about was the significant bulge she'd seen in his swimming trunks.

What was the matter with her?

She *never* thought about things like that.

'You're not very romantic, are you?'

Alex gave a soft laugh. 'I can be very romantic when the need arises.'

'You mean when you want to persuade someone to s-sleep with you,' she stammered, unable to hide her distaste. 'I can't believe women fall for your patter.'

His eyes glittered and he moved towards her with all the graceful stealth of a jungle cat. 'Is that a challenge, Miss Phillips?'

She backed away so fast she almost stumbled, hideously aware of every muscular inch of him. 'No. It certainly isn't. Unlike most of the women you mix with, I know exactly what sort of man you are, Alex Westerling.'

Dangerous.

'So you keep telling me,' he said silkily, 'but you're obviously finding me incredibly hard to resist.'

She gaped at him. 'No wonder you need four cottages to live in! Your ego would never fit into just one. For your information, I don't have any trouble resisting you.'

'No.' He was maddeningly cool and relaxed and there was a hint of laughter in his wicked blue eyes. 'Then why did you bring me the shirt, sweetheart? Go on, admit it. The sight of my body was really disturbing you.'

Her heart was banging against her ribs and she stared at him, dry-mouthed. 'You are the most arrogant, hateful—'

She broke off and he laughed.

'Jenny, you brought me the shirt,' he said mildly. 'You wanted me to cover up.'

Cheeks hot with anger and another emotion that she couldn't identify, Jenny scooped up Daisy and then proceeded to struggle with the rug.

'Here—give me that.' His tone still amused, he took it from her and thrust it under his arm before strolling back across the sand to fetch his shoes.

She fought the impulse to throw something at him and followed him back to the house, glaring at his broad back. She was still simmering when he dropped the rug inside the door, poured himself a drink and disappeared up the stairs to his room without a backward glance.

Frowning after him in total frustration, Jenny made her own way upstairs and prepared Daisy for bed.

Her heart was thumping and she felt hot all over.

'Your father is a total nightmare,' she muttered as she finally tucked the little girl into her cot. 'And I have no idea how we're going to persuade him to take notice of you. Maybe once his lawyer has confirmed the truth he'll start acting in a more responsible manner.'

She lifted a hand and stroked the baby's back gently, smiling as she saw Daisy's eyes close. Just being with the little girl soothed her and she sighed, wishing that she hadn't reacted so strongly to Alex's teasing. And she was sure now that he had been teasing her.

'I suppose he thinks that if he's horrid enough then I'll leave,' she whispered quietly, knowing that the baby wouldn't care what she was saying as long as the voice was suitably restful. 'But we're not going to leave, are we? He's your daddy and he's going to get to know you.'

But she wasn't going to let Alex bait her again.

Satisfied that Daisy was asleep, she made her way downstairs, tensing as she reached the living room. There was no sign of Alex and she assumed that he must be up in his bedroom, changing after his swim.

Jenny walked into the kitchen and gathered together the ingredients that she'd bought earlier.

However tired or angry he was, surely he had to eat some time?

And if they ate together maybe they could establish at least some sort of relationship—that was going to be essential if he was to be part of Daisy's life.

It would have been a great deal easier if they weren't so different, she reflected helplessly, digging around in his kitchen for the equipment she needed.

She heated some oil in a huge wok that she found in one of his cupboards, tossed in some fresh garlic and ginger and then added spring onions. Hopefully the smell would tempt him downstairs.

By the time he appeared in the doorway she'd added strips of chicken and vegetables and everything was sizzling temptingly.

'What the hell do you think you're doing?'

His soft tone made her catch her breath but she stayed outwardly calm, concentrating on draining the noodles instead and adding them to the wok.

'I'm cooking dinner.'

'Very domestic,' he said sardonically. 'I didn't realise that this little agreement of ours included catering. What else is on offer, I wonder?'

She wondered whether he was trying to shock her on purpose.

Determined not to react, Jenny ignored his insinuation and took a deep breath. 'Dr Westerling—Alex—you didn't eat breakfast and to the best of my knowledge you worked through lunch. As you don't seem to have planned anything for dinner either, I thought I'd better prepare something.'

'What makes you think I haven't already planned something for dinner?'

'The contents of your fridge.' She shook the wok and risked a glance in his direction. 'It's full of beer.'

He lifted an eyebrow in blatant mockery. 'What's wrong with that?'

She kept her tone light. 'You can tell a lot about someone from what's in their fridge.'

'Is that right?' He lounged against the doorframe, his blue eyes glittering dangerously. 'And what does my fridge tell you about me?'

'That you don't take care of yourself,' she said bluntly, tossing the contents of the wok with skilful turns of the long-handled metal spatula she'd found. 'You drink too much and you don't eat properly.'

There was an ominous silence.

'Anything else?'

She ignored his sarcastic tone and emptied the contents of the wok onto two plates.

Yes. He had a wicked reputation with women.

But she wasn't bringing that up now, she reminded herself firmly. The atmosphere was already tense enough. If she wanted him to be a father to Daisy then she had to build some sort of relationship with the man, and she wasn't going to do that if she was constantly reminding him that she disapproved of his morals.

Instead, she handed him a plate with a calm smile. 'I hope you like Chinese—I didn't ask you.'

His eyes clashed with hers and then drifted down to the plate.

For a moment she thought he might refuse to eat it but instead his eyes narrowed and his firm mouth lifted at the corners. 'So you want to eat dinner with me—very cosy.'

His voice was silky smooth and he reminded her of a lethal predator tempting his prey into his lair.

Her breath stuck in her throat. 'I have no particular desire to eat dinner with you, Dr Westerling,' she said, struggling to keep her voice steady, 'but seeing as we both have to eat I thought I might as well cook for both of us.'

'We'll eat outside.'

Having delivered that statement, he turned and strode through the living room, clearly expecting her to follow him.

She did so at a slower pace, wondering whether she was actually going to be able to eat anything. Her insides were so churned up that she had a feeling the food might stick in her throat.

She settled herself near the door and his eyes flickered to the intercom that she placed next to her.

'What's that for?'

'It's so that I can hear Daisy.' She lifted her fork and stabbed a piece of broccoli and made an attempt at civilised conversation. 'It's very beautiful here. Do you swim every evening?'

'Yes.' His answer was terse and she gave up on conversation, choosing instead to sit quietly and concentrate on her meal.

It was all very well wanting Alex to get to know Daisy but she was only too aware that it meant that he had to get to know her, too. And he'd made it perfectly clear that she was the last person he'd choose to spend time with. If she hadn't been here she had no doubt that he would be doing something much more exciting than sitting on his deck eating noodles.

They ate in a tense silence for a few minutes more and then she tried again.

'This is a fantastic spot.'

'I chose it for its privacy.' His meaning was crystal clear and she sighed, wondering how she was ever going to build any sort of relationship with him.

The truth was, she just wasn't used to dealing with men like him. He was way out of her league and just being within a metre of the man made her nervous. If it hadn't been for Daisy she would have legged it the moment he'd stepped out of his flashy sports car.

'What's the sauce?'

She jumped, startled that he'd actually spoken to her. 'Pardon?'

'I like the sauce.' He took another mouthful and nodded approvingly. 'It's delicious.'

He liked her cooking?

She hid her surprise. 'I—I made it. It's a mixture of things.'

'Well, it's good.' He lounged back in his chair, his glass in his hand. 'You're very domesticated, aren't you? Home-made bread for breakfast, baby food from scratch, dinner in the evening…'

Jenny flushed, sensing that he was mocking her again. 'I love cooking.'

'Very wifely.'

She winced at his acid comment.

'I'm not trying to be wifely, Dr Westerling,' she replied steadily. 'But both of us have to eat so it seemed sensible for me to cook. You may find this hard to believe but I don't have any designs on you at all.'

Alex cleared his plate and lounged back in his chair. 'I do find it hard to believe,' he said shortly. 'Women have used all sorts of tactics in the past to try and persuade me into marriage, but you're the first one to actually go to the lengths of producing a baby. You'll have to forgive me if I'm a little sceptical about your motives.'

Marriage?

She gaped at him. 'Is that what you think? That I want you to *marry* me?'

He shrugged carelessly. 'Why else would you move in here and start cooking me dinner?'

Marry Alex Westerling? It would mean sentencing herself to a lifetime of torture. She would never, ever be comfortable with him. He was just too…too…*male*.

'I moved in because I want you to get to know Daisy,' she said, utterly appalled by his arrogance, 'and I cooked us dinner because we both have to eat. Believe me, given the choice, the last place I'd want to live is with you and I wouldn't marry you if you paid me.'

Alex yawned. 'Is that right?'

He didn't believe her.

She looked at him in genuine amazement. 'Frankly, I can't understand why so many women are desperate to marry you.' She stabbed a piece of chicken. 'They must be mad.'

Her last comment was muttered under her breath but he heard her and he shot her a look that she couldn't interpret.

'You really wouldn't want to marry me?' There was a strange light in his eyes and she looked at him and shook her head, her shyness temporarily forgotten.

'Absolutely not. You lead a totally selfish lifestyle, you're insufferably arrogant and you've obviously been getting your own way since the day you were born. As a husband you'd be a nightmare.'

There was a silence and then Alex threw his head back and laughed in genuine amusement.

'Oh Jenny, Jenny.' He was still chuckling as he reached forward for his drink. 'Aren't you worried about my poor ego?'

She shot him a look of contempt. 'Your ego is so inflated that I could chip away at it for weeks and not make any impression.'

His eyes were still brimming with humour. 'I'm beginning to think you might be my type after all. Where have you been all my life?'

Jenny felt more and more unsettled. Why didn't his reactions ever match her expectations?

Surely he should have been offended that she didn't want to marry him, not amused.

'I've been avoiding men like you.'

He ran a hand over his rough jaw and she found herself noticing the way the sides of his firm mouth creased when he smiled.

'What I want to know,' he said in that lazy upper-class drawl that was doubtless the product of a vastly expensive education, 'is why, if you find my lifestyle so distasteful, you want me to be Daisy's father. Aren't you worried about my pernicious influence?'

'I don't *want* you to be Daisy's father,' she delivered coolly, giving up on her dinner and placing her fork carefully on the plate. 'I didn't choose you, but apparently my sister did and we have to live with that fact.'

His eyes narrowed. 'You really do believe I'm her father, don't you?'

She stared at him, thinking that it was an odd question.

'Absolutely. Why else would I be here?' She held his gaze. 'Why would my sister lie?'

'I have absolutely no idea,' he replied thoughtfully, 'but I have every intention of finding out.'

With that he stood up and walked away from her, indicating that the conversation was over.

He was like a tiger, she reflected helplessly, watching as he prowled back into his enormous living room and fiddled with the stereo. A solitary male, moving through life on his own, careful never to form a relationship with anyone. Even from her short acquaintance with the man she could see that he never allowed anyone close to him.

Who or what had made him that way?

As far as she was aware, his family was stable enough. His father was one of the richest men in the country and she knew that he'd inherited enormous wealth himself. He certainly didn't have money worries.

In fact, judging from the careless way he lounged on the sofa, eyes closed as he listened to the music, one arm flung across his forehead, he didn't seem to have any worries at all.

Jenny stared at him in helpless frustration.

He was obviously determined to ignore the fact that Daisy was his child.

How on earth was she ever going to encourage him to build a relationship with her?

CHAPTER FOUR

IT WAS the cry that woke him.

Dragged from a deep sleep by the terrified wails, Alex jerked upright in bed and waited for the cries to stop.

They didn't.

He muttered a curse and sprang out of bed, padding barefoot along the landing towards the room he'd had decorated as a nursery.

The baby was sobbing in her cot and Alex frowned, glancing behind him, expecting to see Jenny hurrying to take over.

But there was no sign of Jenny.

Cursing softly under his breath, he stepped into the room and scooped the baby out of the cot, feeling the dampness soaking through her cotton sleepsuit.

He rolled his eyes. 'No wonder you're yelling,' he muttered softly, tucking the baby against his shoulder. 'You need changing. You need your mummy.' He broke off as he said the words, remembering that she no longer had a mother.

But she had Jenny.

Where the hell was Jenny?

He glanced impatiently towards the door again but the landing was still in darkness and there was no sign of movement from the other bedroom.

The baby had stopped crying and was snuffling softly against his neck but he knew that the moment he put her down she'd start crying again, and no wonder. She was soaking wet.

Muttering under his breath, he glanced around the room.

Nappies were neatly stacked next to a changing mat, along with wipes and everything else he was likely to need.

There was no reason why he couldn't change her himself.

Except that it just wasn't the sort of thing he did.

Even with his sisters' children, he avoided the nappies.

He glanced impatiently towards the door again but there was still no sign of Jenny.

For a moment he was tempted to wake her, and then the baby smiled up at him again and for the first time in his life Alex Westerling found himself utterly captivated by a female.

Her soft, baby smile warmed something deep inside him, reaching a part of himself that he hadn't known existed.

Staring down into her gorgeous blue eyes, Alex decided that maybe they didn't need Jenny's help after all.

He dealt with life-threatening situations on a daily basis.

He could deal with one wet nappy.

'OK, young lady, I suppose we'll have to do this ourselves, but you're going to have to be patient. This whole nappy business is new to me. Whenever my sisters visit with their offspring, I always avoid this bit.' He laid her gently on the mat on the floor and undid her sleepsuit. 'Ugh. This is totally disgusting. No wonder you were screaming.'

He tossed the damp sleepsuit on the floor with an exclamation of distaste and glanced towards the bathroom.

'I'm going to be right back—don't move.' He straightened up and walked into the bathroom, wetting a flannel and picking up a towel. By the time he returned the baby had rolled off the mat and was kicking happily on the carpet.

Alex laughed softly. 'Think you're clever, do you? Drying yourself off on my carpet.' He knelt down, lifted her back onto the changing mat and gently washed her while she gurgled and tried to grab his face with her tiny hands. 'Keep still. You're dealing with a total amateur.'

Finally he was satisfied that she was dry and reached for a nappy, opening it up and looking at it doubtfully.

'Which way up does this thing go? Have you any idea?' He pulled a face at the baby who chuckled and clapped her hands. 'Stop laughing. Tapes at the front or tapes at the back?'

He experimented, decided which was correct and then tried to slip it under Daisy's bottom, but she'd decided that this was a great game and proceeded to twist and wriggle until he grunted with frustration.

'For crying out loud, baby,' he growled, wincing as the tapes stuck themselves to the hair on his arms for the third time. 'Ouch! This is worse than sticky plasters. Thank goodness my sisters Katy and Libby can't see me now. I'd never hear the last of it. Just lie still, will you? Don't you know a beginner when you see one?'

Finally he managed to secure the nappy and dress her in a clean sleepsuit.

'There. You're dry now.' He picked her up and she snuggled against him, her eyes drifting shut immediately.

Alex looked down at her and sucked in a breath. She looked utterly defenceless.

'You poor scrap. You've lost your mother and no one seems to know who your father is,' he murmured, stroking her head softly as he supported her. 'I honestly don't think it's me but we're trying to find out for sure and if it is— well, I suppose we'll come to some agreement. Try not to worry. At least you've got your Aunty Jenny and she seems pretty good at homely things. She makes your food from scratch and I'm sure it's very healthy—even though it does look disgusting.'

He wondered why Jenny hadn't woken up. Maybe she was exhausted. It occurred to him that she must have had a very tough six months, what with losing her sister and being landed with a baby that wasn't hers.

No wonder she was looking for help.

He settled the baby in the cot and watched her sleep, his expression suddenly thoughtful.

He'd always thought that having a baby would be just about the worst thing in the world but suddenly he wasn't so sure.

There was certainly nothing horrifying about Daisy.

She was incredibly sweet.

Shocked by his own thoughts, he swore softly and raked long fingers through his dark hair.

What the hell was happening to him?

Babies were not sweet. Babies marked a very definite end to a bachelor existence and a start to a lifetime of self-sacrifice.

It wasn't a route he intended to take.

Jenny stood in the corridor, hardly daring to breathe.

She'd been woken by the first cry but then it had occurred to her that this was a golden opportunity to force Alex closer to Daisy. Surely he wouldn't be able to ignore the baby's cries?

And he hadn't.

She'd stayed in her room, suppressing the natural urge to rush to the baby, biting her nails until she'd heard his heavy tread on the landing and his rough male voice talking to Daisy.

She had no idea what he'd done but Daisy had stopped crying so whatever it was had obviously worked.

And he was still in her room.

Not sure whether that was a good thing or not, Jenny crept back to her room and slid into bed.

Hopefully, exposing Alex to the baby would improve their relationship, but on the other hand it was a strategy that could totally backfire. Alex was a hardened bachelor who valued his independence above everything. Spending too much time with Daisy could just reinforce his prejudices about the effects of babies on his lifestyle.

He could decide that he wanted nothing to do with Daisy. And then what would she do?

Jenny was downstairs giving Daisy breakfast the next morning when Alex strode into the kitchen full of purpose.

'Get Daisy's things together. We're going shopping.'

Jenny paused with the spoon halfway to Daisy's mouth. 'Sorry?'

'Shopping.' He glanced round the kitchen expectantly. 'Is there any of that delicious coffee?'

Jenny blinked, registering the fact that he thought her coffee was delicious. 'It's on the side,' she said warily, wondering what was going on. 'What are we going shopping for?'

'Toys.' He helped himself to coffee and stared at the freshly baked batch of rolls cooling on a rack in the centre of the table. 'Are those spare?'

His tone was casual and she hid a smile. 'Help yourself.'

She felt a thrill of satisfaction that she'd finally persuaded him to eat breakfast. 'Why are we shopping for toys?'

'Because Daisy doesn't have any.'

Jenny stared at him, unable to hide her amazement. 'You want to buy Daisy some *toys*?'

He didn't look at her, instead reaching for a roll and covering it in butter and honey. 'Every child needs toys. I know a great toy shop. I take my nieces and nephews there. We'll go there and find something for Daisy.'

Still flabbergasted by his sudden interest, Jenny hesitated. Should she remind him that at six months a baby didn't need much in the way of toys? No. Any interest from him was surely to be encouraged.

'But why?' She nibbled her lip, unable to comprehend

his sudden interest in the baby. 'You don't think Daisy's your child.'

'I'm sure she isn't.' He poured himself some coffee. 'But that doesn't mean I can't buy her toys. The kid's had a rough time.'

Had a rough time?

Jenny looked at him curiously, considerably heartened by the fact that he at least seemed sympathetic to Daisy's situation.

That had to be a good thing. It would make him more likely to help when his lawyers confirmed her parentage.

'If that's what you want,' she said, and he nodded, biting into the roll with a grunt of approval.

'You're a good cook.'

Not used to receiving praise, Jenny coloured and concentrated on Daisy. 'Thank you.'

'OK, here's what we're going to do.' He finished the roll and reached for his coffee. 'I can see that life must have been tough for you over the past six months and I'm willing to help you until we can find out who Daisy's father is.'

Jenny opened her mouth to point out that she knew that it was *him* and then closed it again. She had no wish to antagonise him and he obviously had it all worked out.

There'd be time enough for him to take full responsibility when his lawyers found out the truth.

'You can stay here until you find her father. Once we trace the guy I'll get my lawyers to sort it all out so that you have decent financial support for Daisy.'

He obviously felt he was being extraordinarily generous and Jenny sighed.

'It isn't just about financial support, Dr Westerling.'

'Alex,' he prompted immediately, and she gave a brief smile.

'Alex. It isn't about money. Most of all I want Daisy to have a father. It's really important for a little girl to know her daddy. I had such a great relationship with my dad when I was growing up. He was such an important part of my life. I don't want Daisy to be denied that.'

Alex gave a humourless laugh. 'Better find out what sort of person the father is before you commit Daisy to a relationship,' he advised, his tone suddenly harsh. 'If he's anything like my father, she'd be better off on her own.'

Jenny looked at him, sensing his sudden tension. 'Why? What was your father like?'

His expression was suddenly blank, all evidence of emotion gone. 'I have no intention of discussing him with you. Just because I'm prepared to help you, it doesn't mean I intend to start spilling my guts. Not my style.'

'You prefer to drink and work and lose yourself in blonde women whose names you can't remember,' Jenny shot back, and then bit her lip. 'Sorry.'

To her surprise Alex laughed, some of the tension leaving his broad shoulders. 'Ouch. There you go again, forgetting your manners—but as it happens you're absolutely right. Do you have a problem with that?'

Heart thumping, Jenny tried to look away but her eyes were trapped by the wicked gleam in his.

'I—I just think there are b-better ways of relaxing,' she stammered quickly, and he flashed her a smile that made her realise immediately why women fell into his bed so easily.

'If you think that,' he drawled softly, 'then you've obviously never had really good sex.'

Her face turned a fiery red and she couldn't think of a single suitable retort.

Alex Westerling was used to dealing with sophisticated women and she was anything but sophisticated.

She could just imagine his amusement if he discovered that she'd never even had a proper boyfriend.

She concentrated on feeding Daisy and hoped he'd drop the subject.

He didn't.

'I can't make you out, Jenny Phillips.' He spoke in that lazy, masculine drawl that seemed to connect with her nerve endings. 'Are you really as innocent as you appear? Every time I mention sex you turn the colour of a fire engine.'

Oh, help.

'My sex life is none of your business, Dr Westerling,'

His eyes gleamed. 'Perhaps I'm levelling the playing field. You seem to take a keen interest in my sex life so I don't see why you should escape unscathed.'

'I'm only interested in your relationship with my sister,' Jenny said in a strangled voice, wondering how this conversation had started. She really, *really* didn't want to be talking about sex with Alex Westerling.

It was conjuring up images that she found incredibly disturbing.

Alex smiled. 'All right, Little Red Riding Hood. We'll leave it at that for now, but just remember—if you expect privacy yourself, it pays to afford others the same courtesy.'

Vowing never to ask him anything personal again, Jenny changed the subject hastily. 'Why do you call me Little Red Riding Hood?'

He leaned forward, his blue eyes faintly mocking. 'Because you arrive at Grandma's cottage, knock trustingly on the door, clutching your freshly baked rolls, and don't notice the wolf,' he said softly, and Jenny caught her breath at the look in his eyes.

She'd never met a man with such wicked, laughing eyes. They seemed to tease and seduce at the same time.

'I—I noticed the wolf,' she stammered, her fingers shaking slightly as she held the spoon. 'But I know he would never be interested in me. Or I in him.'

His eyes held hers for a long moment and then slid down, surveying every inch of her before returning to her shocked face. 'Is that right?'

For an endless, breathless moment of aching intensity

their eyes held and then Daisy bashed her spoon on the table and Jenny was jerked back to the present.

What was she doing?

And what was *he* doing?

She knew she wasn't his type, and he certainly wasn't hers.

Was he just trying to make her uneasy? If so then he'd definitely succeeded.

Thoroughly flustered by feelings that she couldn't identify, Jenny wiped Daisy's mouth and scooped her out of the high chair.

'About this shopping…'

Alex rose to his feet in a fluid movement and reached for his car keys. 'We'll go as soon as you're ready. I'll put her car seat in my car.'

Refraining from asking how he was going to fit a baby seat in his flashy sports car, Jenny concentrated on Daisy, gathering together a selection of things that they might need for the trip.

Still thoroughly unsettled by the conversation over breakfast, she would have done anything to avoid more close contact with him, but as this was the first real interest he'd shown in Daisy she didn't want to reject his offer.

It would be fine, she told herself firmly as she carried Daisy out to the car.

He hadn't meant anything by his comments.

He'd just been teasing her.

She knew for a fact that she wasn't his type. And he certainly wasn't hers.

She had absolutely nothing to worry about.

Three hours later Alex handed over his credit card with a satisfied smile.

At least now it couldn't be said that Daisy didn't have toys.

'Thank you, Dr Westerling,' the assistant said smoothly,

eyeing the enormous bill with the smug satisfaction of someone who received a bonus on sales. 'Will there be anything else?'

Anything else?

Alex flashed him a look of intense irritation and refrained from pointing out that he'd already bought half the shop. He pocketed his credit card and glanced benignly at the object of his largesse.

Daisy was sleeping soundly in her pushchair, oblivious to the fact that she was now the proud owner of several dolls complete with changes of clothes, stuffed toys, rattles, chunky bricks and a baby gym guaranteed to turn every child into a genius.

Alex gathered up the bags, noticing that Jenny was looking at the toys, the floor, the ceiling—in fact, anywhere but at him.

And that was totally his fault, of course.

Ever since that conversation at breakfast when he'd mentioned their sex lives, she'd avoided eye contact.

He gritted his teeth.

He hadn't intended to embarrass her but frankly he didn't know any girls of her age who were embarrassed about sex. They seemed to talk about it quite freely.

But not Jenny, obviously.

Little Red Riding Hood.

He let out a sigh as they strolled back to the car, wondering what he had to do to make her relax with him again. She obviously had him pegged as a real seducer of women. After the way he'd teased her at breakfast she was probably worrying about her virtue.

And she really didn't need to.

As she'd rightly pointed out, she wasn't his type.

He always went for blondes.

Reminding himself of that fact, he took Daisy from her but found himself looking at Jenny, noticing the thickness of her dark lashes and the smoothness of her cheeks.

It didn't matter what her colouring was, he told himself firmly, strapping Daisy into her seat. The main reason that he wasn't interested in her was because she was so obviously different from the sort of women that he usually spent time with.

Jenny didn't do casual sex.

You only had to witness her appalled reaction to his lifestyle to know that.

He shocked her, and Alex didn't tangle with women who were easily shocked.

Keeping his eyes on the road, Alex waited for her to strap herself in and then hit the accelerator.

This whole business was stressing him out and the sooner his lawyers identified Daisy's real father, then the better for all of them.

Jenny was relieved when Monday came.

She was finding it harder and harder to relax around Alex.

Everything about him was aggressively masculine, from the way he always took command of every situation to the way he lay sprawled on one of his sofas, watching cricket on his wide-screen TV or listening to music through headphones.

She'd thought that she wanted Alex to spend more time with Daisy but what she hadn't considered was that spending time with Daisy inevitably meant spending time with him. And being forced into close contact with Alex Westerling for the best part of two whole days had left her feeling decidedly unsettled. Even though she knew he couldn't possibly be interested in her, she couldn't forget his comment about her walking into the wolf's lair.

But at least he'd started to show an interest in Daisy.

The day before, he'd insisted that they all go to the beach and he'd carried the little girl into the sea, dangling her feet in the water until she'd chortled with laughter. Jenny had watched quietly from her position on the sand, a lump in her throat as she'd seen Alex smile indulgently as the little girl had kicked her legs and splashed him.

When she'd nervously cooked dinner he'd reined in the sarcastic comments and merely complimented her on her cooking.

In fact, he'd proved to be such entertaining company over dinner that she'd had to forcibly remind herself that he was the same man who had seduced Chloe and then left her.

All in all the whole weekend had left her feeling increasingly confused and unsettled. Before she'd turned up on his doorstep she'd thought she'd known exactly the sort of man Alex Westerling was. Now she wasn't so sure.

Fortunately she was prevented from dwelling on the situation by the arrival of an ambulance.

'Little boy tried to run in front of a car,' the paramedic told her as he pushed the trolley into the main area of the A and E department. 'Mother managed to grab hold of him but he fell and hit his face on the pavement. He's going to have a nasty black eye.'

Jenny glanced up as a young woman rushed into the department, dragging a toddler behind her and carrying a baby. She looked unbelievably upset and harassed.

'I just can't believe he did that.' She pressed a hand to her chest, her breath coming in gasps. 'One minute I was in the bank cashing a cheque, and the next minute he just grinned at me and dashed out of the door as if it was all a big game. I only just stopped him from going into the road and there was this lorry…'

She closed her eyes tightly and Jenny winced, experiencing the same mental images as the mother.

If she hadn't caught up with the child—

'Try not to think about what might have happened,' Jenny said hastily, taking the woman's arm and guiding her into Resus. 'I'm sure he's going to be fine. I'll just take some details from you and then we'll ask a doctor to see him.'

The woman was battling with tears. 'It's just too much.' She broke off and rubbed a hand over her face. 'He's such a monkey. He's always in trouble and I've been up all night with the baby and you only have to turn your back for a minute and he gets himself into trouble.'

'Some children are like that,' Jenny agreed, her tone sympathetic. She settled the little boy on the trolley and listened while the paramedic gave her the rest of the details.

The mother hurried over to the trolley and hugged the child with her free arm, tears spilling out of her eyes. 'How many times have I told you that you don't run away from Mummy?'

The little boy's face crumpled and he started to sob miserably.

Jenny said a hasty thank you to the paramedic and hurried over to the trolley to try and help.

'OK.' Her voice was calm and steady and she smiled at the toddler. 'What have you been up to, mischief? You've frightened the life out of your mum.'

She filled his details on a card and then checked his obs.

'He hasn't been unwell at all, Mrs Newton? No temperature or anything?'

'Please, call me Helen, and, no, he hasn't been ill.' She frowned slightly. 'Why do you ask?'

'Because when children fall we need to be sure that there isn't something else going on,' Jenny told her. 'Sometimes an ear infection might cause him to lose his balance.'

'He just tripped because he was running away from me,' Helen said tightly, and Jenny nodded.

'And are you're sure he wasn't knocked out?'

Helen shook her head. 'No. He howled immediately so I know he was conscious.'

'OK, well, I need to ask a doctor to check him over,' Jenny told her, scribbling on the notes. She glanced up and noticed that Helen had her eyes closed and was breathing slowly. 'Are you all right?'

Helen gave a wan smile. 'Not really, but I don't suppose anyone is with three children under five and the amount of sleep I get. I'm fine really. Just tired and unfit. I was so breathless after I chased after Jack and it was only a few feet.'

Jenny smiled. 'You can't be that unfit if you're chasing round after these three all day.'

'Well, I am.' Helen hurried over to her little girl who was tugging at one of the cupboards in Resus. 'Stop that, Bella! Come and sit down.' She sighed and cast Jenny an apologetic look. 'Sorry. Controlling them is a nightmare. It's no wonder I get chest pains.'

'Chest pains?' Jenny frowned, but before she could question her further, Alex strolled in, broad-shouldered and a vision of unshakable confidence.

Awareness slammed through her and she looked away quickly, shocked by the intensity of her own reaction.

What had happened to her over the last few days?

Had she lost every bit of common sense?

Despite everything she knew about Alex Westerling, he still made her heart beat faster and her breathing stop.

Which just proved that she was as vulnerable to his lethal charm as every other member of her sex.

Horrified by the realisation that he could affect her so strongly, she stared at him stupidly and he lifted an eyebrow in her direction.

'Tina mentioned that you needed a doctor in here.'

'Yes.' Jenny croaked the word out and waved a hand towards the trolley. 'This is Jack. He fell and hit his head on the kerb. He wasn't knocked out and his GCS is 15.'

Alex strolled over to the trolley and smiled at the little boy. 'Hello, there, Jack. That's a pretty impressive eye you've got there.'

Helen groaned. 'Don't tell him that, he'll do it again.'

Alex grinned. 'He's a boy. He's bound to do it again, only next time it'll probably be someone's fist rather than the pavement.' He turned back to the little boy. 'I just need to have a little feel of your head, is that OK?'

Jenny watched him with grudging admiration. She didn't want him to be a good doctor. She really didn't. But he was.

And he had a nice way with children.

She watched while he examined Jack, chatting easily to him about subjects that she wouldn't have expected him to know about, like Thomas the Tank Engine and Bob the Builder.

Bob the Builder?

What did Alex Westerling know about Bob the Builder?

He reached for an ophthalmoscope and examined Jack's eyes, one large hand steadying the child's head as he altered the angle.

'Well, that looks OK.' He ran his fingers around the bony orbit of the eye, checking that it was intact. Then he turned to Helen. 'I don't think he's done himself serious damage. The bruising should improve gradually. Obviously he had a bang on his head so you'll need to keep an eye on him for twenty-four hours. Any sickness or headache—anything at all you're worried about—bring him back in or call your GP. Jenny will give you a form that explains everything.'

He chatted for a moment longer and then left the room. Jenny reached for a head injury form, watching as Helen walked over to extract her little girl from the cupboard for the second time.

She was wearing shorts and Jenny noticed that her left leg seemed swollen.

Was it her imagination?

She looked closer and decided that it wasn't. Helen's leg was definitely swollen.

'Helen…' She hesitated, unsure how to voice her concerns.

'Your leg seems a little swollen. Is that usual for you?'

Helen dragged the little girl out of the cupboard, her expression harassed. 'No, but the weather's been hot and I'm on my feet all day.'

Jenny chewed her lip. It was possible that the heat was the reason, but still...

'The chest pain you mentioned having when you chased after Jack—have you ever had that before?'

'For the last few days.' Helen scooped the little girl into her arms and walked back towards the trolley, holding the squirming toddler. 'I've had a cough so I presumed it was related to that.'

'What sort of cough?' Alarm bells were ringing in Jenny's head.

'Just a cough.' Helen gave a rueful smile. 'I'm a smoker so that's probably got something to do with it.'

'How many do you smoke?'

'About thirty a day, but don't tell my husband.' Helen gave a tired smile. 'You'd smoke too if you were looking after these three.'

'I'm not judging you, Helen,' Jenny assured her quickly. 'I'm just worried about you. Would you mind if I just take a look at your leg?'

Helen looked startled. 'You want to take a look at me? But it's Jack who's had the accident.'

'I know that, but I'm slightly concerned about the symptoms you're describing.'

Helen looked at her. 'You don't think I'm just run down?'

'Possibly, but I'd like to be sure.' Jenny pulled up a chair. 'Sit down there for a moment.'

Helen sat with the toddler on her lap while Jenny examined the leg.

'Does it hurt if I press here?'

Helen winced. 'Yes.'

'Are you taking the Pill, Helen?'

The woman nodded. 'Yes. Why? What's that got to do with my legs and my cough?'

'Maybe nothing,' Jenny admitted, 'but I'm going to ask a doctor to look at you anyway. I've got one more question. Have you ever coughed up any blood?'

'A bit.' Helen was starting to look alarmed. 'I just assumed it was because I coughed too hard.'

'That was probably it,' Jenny agreed, rising to her feet and making for the door. 'Stay there, Helen. I'll be back in a minute.'

She walked briskly into the department and searched for Alex.

He was checking a set of X-rays for one of the more junior doctors.

'You can see a fracture if you look.' He pushed another film into the light-box. 'You were looking at the wrong view.'

'Alex.' Jenny's tone was urgent and he tilted his dark head in her direction, his eyes still fixed on the X-ray.

'What's the matter?'

'It's Helen. The mother of that little boy you just saw.'

'What about her?'

'I'm worried about her. I think she might have a pulmonary embolus.' The moment the words left her mouth she felt stupid. She wasn't a doctor, for goodness' sake. She shouldn't be going around making diagnoses. She waited for him to laugh or say something cutting, but he didn't.

Instead, he abandoned the X-ray and turned towards her, giving her his full attention. 'What are her symptoms?'

Grateful to him for taking her seriously, she swallowed and brushed a strand of hair out of her eyes. 'She's breathless, she has chest pain and she's coughed up blood. She's got some pitting oedema of her right leg and ankle and some tenderness in her right calf.'

Alex stared at her. 'How the hell did you find all that out? She wasn't even the patient.'

Jenny blushed. 'She happened to mention that she became breathless when she ran after Jack to try and stop him going on the road and I noticed that one leg was swollen. If she hadn't been wearing shorts I don't suppose I'd have noticed. It may be nothing…'

'Doesn't sound like nothing to me. Let me just finish off here and I'll be with you.' Alex yanked the X-ray out of the light-box and handed it to the other doctor, who was still hovering. 'Send this guy to fracture clinic for a below-knee plaster and refer him to the orthopaedic lot for follow-up.' He turned to Jenny. 'Let's take a look at your patient.'

She hurried to keep up with him as he strode towards Resus. 'She's a smoker—thirty a day—and she's on the Pill.'

He turned to her with a wry smile, pausing with one hand on the door of Resus. 'Is there anything you didn't find out about her?'

Jenny returned the smile tentatively, thinking that he shouldn't be allowed to smile. It made him dangerously attractive. 'I only asked a few questions…'

'But all the right ones,' he observed softly, his blue eyes suddenly intent. 'Come on, let's see if you're suspicions are right.'

He pushed open the door of Resus and walked over to Helen. 'I gather you've not been feeling too great yourself, Mrs Newton.'

Helen was trying to control the wriggling toddler while reading a book to the other child. 'Well, that's true, but I must admit I just thought it was because of these three. They're hardly relaxing.'

'I can imagine.' Alex scooped the little girl into his arms and looked at Jenny. 'Could you nip and get some toys from the paeds area? These little ones have been here long enough and they're bored stiff. Let's give them something to play with other than surgical instruments, shall we?'

Jenny smiled and hurried off to do as he'd suggested, thinking that for a man who didn't want children he was remarkably sensitive to their needs.

She returned with the toys to find Alex examining Helen's leg. 'Does this hurt?'

Helen pulled a face. 'A bit. Nothing dramatic.'

Alex nodded and his eyes flickered to Jenny. 'I want to get a line in.'

Judging from the urgency of his tone, he obviously agreed with her diagnosis and she reacted immediately, reaching for a venflon and a swab.

Alex squatted down next to Helen who was still sitting on the chair, occupying the toddler.

'Helen, I think it's very likely that you've developed a clot in one of the veins in your leg,' he said gently. 'We call it a DVT. Deep-vein thrombosis. I also think that the clot may have moved up to your lungs, which is why you're coughing. I want to run some tests.'

Helen stared at him. 'You mean stay in hospital?'

'For now, yes.' Alex took the tourniquet that Jenny handed him and slid it over Helen's arm. 'I'm going to put a cannula into your vein so that we can take blood and give you drugs if the need arises.'

He swabbed the back of her hand and then selected a vein and slid the venflon in with practised ease.

'OK.' He straightened and tossed the debris onto the trolley. 'I want a chest X-ray, an ECG and an ultrasound of that leg.'

Jenny hurried off to make the necessary arrangements and Alex called the medical team.

'I can't stay in hospital,' Helen fretted, reaching down to pick up a toy that the little girl had dropped. 'I've got three children under the age of five, one of them with a banged head.'

Jenny glanced at Jack who was lying on the trolley, playing quietly with a toy car.

'Is there anyone we can phone?'

Helen sighed and tipped her head back. 'My husband, I suppose, but he won't thank me.'

Alex walked back over to her, his phone call finished. 'Why won't he thank you?'

'He's got a very busy job,' Helen muttered, concentrating on the children. 'He hates being called when he's working.'

Jenny caught Alex's eye and hid her surprise at his obvious disapproval. Somehow she would have expected him to empathise with a businessman who didn't have time for his children, but again it seemed that she'd misjudged him.

'Jenny will call him,' Alex said smoothly. 'She's good at reminding people of their responsibilities.'

Jenny caught the gleam of amusement in his blue eyes and glared at him.

'I'll be happy to call him,' she said, delivering a sweet smile in Alex's direction. 'I'm sure he'll be only too happy to come at once when he knows that you need him.'

Helen didn't look convinced but at that moment a radiographer hurried into the room, along with two ECG technicians.

Alex gave a brisk nod. 'Great. Let's move you up onto a trolley, Helen, next to Jack. Jenny will take the other two for a little walk while we do the X-rays.'

Noticing that little Bella was showing more than a passing interest in the metal drip stand, Jenny nodded her agreement and gently took the baby from Helen.

'I'm not sure if she'll go with you,' Helen fretted, releasing the baby reluctantly. 'She's terrible with people she doesn't know.'

'She'll be fine with Jenny. Jenny's great with babies,' Alex said immediately, signing the form that the radiographer handed him. 'Babies love her.'

Jenny blinked at the unexpected praise and lifted the baby gently against her shoulder.

Fortunately the baby did seem to love her. Or at least it didn't protest at being cuddled by a total stranger.

Assuring Helen that she'd bring the baby back at the first signs of distress, Jenny left Resus and walked down to the paediatric area to find a phone and look for more distractions.

Still holding the baby, she showed Bella a box of toys and watched with satisfaction as she involved herself with a train set.

Then she called Helen's husband, choosing her words carefully so that he understood the seriousness of the situation.

'Who's this?' Tina strolled up to her as she replaced the phone. 'Shall I call you a doctor to take a look at her?'

Jenny shook her head. 'Nothing wrong with the baby,' she said, and quickly explained what had happened.

Tina's eyes widened. 'You spotted that?'

Jenny blushed. 'Well, I was just—'

'Quick off the mark,' a very male voice interjected from behind them, and Jenny turned to find Alex lounging in the doorway.

Her pulse rate doubled. 'How is she?'

'She has a pulmonary embolus and the medical team is looking at her now.'

'Oh, so it was something—' She broke off and he gave a wry smile.

'It was rather more than *something*, Nurse Phillips. If you hadn't noticed her symptoms, she might well have died.'

Unaccountably warmed by his praise, Jenny cuddled the baby closer. 'Well, I'm glad she's all right.'

Alex pulled a face. 'She's worrying herself silly about the children. Did you get hold of the husband?'

Jenny nodded. 'He's coming straight away. He was very worried.'

'Was he, indeed?' Alex laughed. 'Then you obviously did a good job.' He looked at the baby who was snuggled contentedly against her shoulder. 'Perhaps you'd better take the kids back into her. The medical reg is just seeing her now. He's going to admit her for anticoagulation and observation.'

'Right, well, her husband said he'd be here in the next fifteen minutes so at least he'll be able to take the children.'

Jenny walked with Alex back to Resus and found the medical reg making arrangements to transfer Helen to the ward.

Fortunately her husband arrived quickly and was able to help with the children.

Alex let out a long breath as the doors of Resus swung closed behind them. 'Maybe now we can snatch a quick cup of coffee.'

Jenny glanced at her watch and realised that they'd missed both coffee and lunch but before she could comment the doors swung open again and Tina hurried in, followed by a team of paramedics pushing a trolley.

Alex's gaze flickered to Jenny. 'Obviously no coffee,' he drawled, and she gave a smile of mutual understanding as she hurried to help with the man on the trolley.

It was obviously going to be one of those days.

CHAPTER FIVE

JENNY was just returning the casserole to the oven when she heard Alex's key in the door.

Her heart rate increased and she took a deep breath, bracing herself for more confrontation.

She'd hesitated before making dinner but in the end she'd decided to go ahead.

Doubtless he'd make some caustic comment about the fact that she was behaving like a wife, but she hadn't eaten all day and she knew that he hadn't either. It seemed ridiculous not to eat dinner together.

She looked up to see him standing in the doorway to the kitchen.

'Hi.' She knew she sounded nervous and hated herself for it. 'I cooked dinner because I thought you might be hungry but I'm not trying to be wifely and if you'd rather not then—'

'I'm starving.'

'Oh.' She relaxed slightly and gave him a hesitant smile. 'Well, that's good. It will be about half an hour. I've already bathed Daisy and put her to bed.'

'No hurry.' He lifted a lean hand and yanked at his tie. 'I'll be on the deck.'

Drinking, no doubt.

Jenny watched with a frown as he strolled out of the kitchen. She knew for a fact that he'd had a long and stressful day, but still...

On impulse she followed him through to the living room and hesitated, watching as he poured himself a whisky.

His tie had been discarded and his shirt was now unbuttoned at the neck, revealing a hint of tanned skin covered in curling dark hairs.

He was disturbingly attractive and suddenly she felt strange inside.

'You know, there are other ways of relaxing apart from drinking.'

The moment she'd said the words she wished she could retract them but it was too late.

He was still for a moment and then turned slowly to face her. 'Sorry?'

'I—I just think you drink too much,' she stammered, taking a step backwards as she suddenly became the focus of his attention. 'It isn't good for you.'

The atmosphere was suddenly chilly. 'And since when did my drinking habits become any of your business?'

'You're Daisy's father,' she said simply. 'That makes it my business.'

He gritted his teeth. 'I don't need this, Jenny. I've had a long day. If I want to drink, I'll drink.'

'There are better ways of relaxing.'

He lifted an eyebrow mockingly. 'Just what exactly are you suggesting, Red Riding Hood?' he drawled softly, stepping closer to her.

'I just meant that you could take a bath.' She swallowed. 'Or something like that.'

He studied her in amazed silence. 'A *bath*? You think a bath would relax me?'

His eyes glittered dangerously and she wished immediately that she hadn't suggested the bath. Suddenly her mind was filled with all sorts of disturbing visions of Alex naked.

Ever since she'd seen him in swimming trunks, the image of his body had been imprinted on her mind and the image disturbed her in ways that she couldn't comprehend. She didn't usually notice men in that way. And she didn't want to notice Alex.

'It's what I always do when I've had a bad day,' she

said quickly, taking a step backwards. 'I light candles and have a bath…'

His gaze never wavered from hers. 'Do you, now? Come to think of it, I think it sounds like a great idea.' He moved towards her. 'Let's go.'

Her breathing stopped. 'L-let's go?'

'Certainly.' His smile was almost devilish and she felt goose-bumps break out on her skin. He was wickedly handsome and it was absolutely impossible to look away from those blue eyes. They seemed to strip away all her defences and leave her emotionally naked before him.

'Dr Westerling—Alex…' Her voice was little more than a croak and his eyes slid down her body with a thoroughness that left her struggling for air.

'I'm more than willing to try your alternative form of relaxation.'

'Y-you're being ridiculous,' she stammered. 'You know I didn't mean that.'

'You propositioned me.'

'I—I didn't.'

'You were the one who suggested the bath,' he said silkily, and she rubbed damp palms down the seams of her jeans, knowing that he was teasing her. He had to be teasing her.

'You know I didn't mean it *that* way.'

He lifted an eyebrow and moved closer still. 'How do I know that?'

Her heart was thumping so fast she felt as though it was going to burst out of her chest. 'Well, for a start because I'm not your type.'

He shrugged carelessly. 'It's true that generally I prefer blondes, but you'll do fine. You've got a great body.'

She flushed and looked away from him. 'It isn't fair of you to tease me.'

There was a long silence. 'Tease you?' There was a sharp

edge to his tone, all traces of mockery gone. 'What makes you think I was teasing you?'

Because she knew she didn't have a good body.

'Look—can we, please, change the subject?' She was squirming with embarrassment and, as usual, he looked totally relaxed.

'No, we can't.' He was frowning now. 'I want to know why you think I'm teasing you.'

She gave a sigh of exasperation. 'Because I'm small and flat-chested and even a push-up bra can't give me a cleavage. I don't have a great body by anyone's standards but that doesn't mean I enjoy being teased about it.'

For a moment he stood still and then she felt his hands slide round her face and he tilted her head until she was forced to look at him.

'I wasn't teasing you. You have a great body,' he said quietly. 'Incredibly delicate and feminine. The only problem is in your head. Someone has obviously made you feel unattractive. Are you going to tell me who?'

She pulled away from him, totally flustered. He thought she had a great body? *Alex Westerling thought she had a great body?* No one had ever paid her a compliment before and she didn't know how to react. Especially when it came from a man she was supposed to despise.

'Please—let's just forget it.'

There was another silence and then he smiled, the mockery back.

'I thought you wanted me to scrub your back in the bath.'

'That wasn't what I was suggesting, and you know it,' she muttered, wishing that she was immune to him. She wanted to be. Oh, she really, really wanted to be, but it seemed that she was as susceptible to that killer smile as the rest of the female population.

He folded his arms across his broad chest and smiled. 'You could teach me how to relax.'

She was thoroughly flustered and he knew it. 'I didn't mean—'

He gave a soft laugh. 'Then take some advice. Don't play with fire, Jenny. And don't try and reform me.'

With that he drained his drink, his eyes never leaving hers, challenging her to comment.

She didn't.

She was too busy trying to work out why Alex had such a powerful effect on her. He was everything she avoided in a man.

But just being in the same room as him had an alarming effect on her pulse rate and she was achingly aware of his powerful physique and his overwhelming masculinity.

'I'd better check on Daisy,' she croaked finally, desperate to get away from him.

'Coward.' His soft laugh followed her as she hurried up the stairs and sought refuge in Daisy's bedroom.

She curled her fingers round the cot rail and closed her eyes briefly. She didn't know how to cope with his banter. She wasn't any good at clever retorts and she was hopeless at flirting. That had been Chloe's forte. Aware that she couldn't lurk in Daisy's room for ever, she slid into the bathroom, tidied her hair and then went back down to the kitchen to finish off the dinner.

'I shouldn't tease you. I'm sorry.' Alex's voice came from behind her and she turned, startled.

'That's all right.'

'No, it isn't all right.' He gave a wry smile. 'The truth is, I'm not used to women like you, Jenny Phillips. You don't flirt—in fact, you don't play any of the games that women usually play. I know that I shock you and some wicked part of me seems to need to see how far I can go before you slap my face.'

'You're pretty safe.' She gave a hesitant smile. 'I hate violence.'

He laughed. 'I bet you do. You're the most placid person I've ever met. Do you ever lose your temper?'

'It isn't one of my vices.'

'You have vices?' He shot her a disbelieving look and she smiled.

'Of course I do.'

'All right, name one.' He sounded thoroughly sceptical and she lifted the casserole out of the oven and placed it on the table.

'Chocolate.'

Alex groaned. 'Not another one. What is it with women and chocolate? My sister Libby can't live without chocolate. Chocolate and shoes.'

'She sounds nice.' Jenny put the plates on the table. 'Is she the one with the children?' She blushed and bit her lip. 'Sorry, I know you said you don't want to talk about your family…'

Alex shrugged. 'That was when we were strangers.' He sat down at the table and reached for some bread. 'We're not exactly strangers any more, are we?'

Jenny served the casserole, wondering what was happening to her emotions.

She'd arrived here full of anger and hatred for the man and somehow here they were, eating dinner in a relatively amicable fashion.

But if she was ever going to persuade him to take an interest in Daisy then they had to be amicable, she reasoned, handing him a plate and pushing a bowl of freshly cooked vegetables towards him.

'Libby has two little girls of four and two, and my other sister Katy has five-year-old twins—a boy and a girl. Multiple births run in the family, it seems.' Alex spooned some vegetables onto his plate. 'We're triplets but I expect you already know that if you read the papers. My sisters used to feature regularly until they married. Then the press seemed to lose interest.'

'And now it's all concentrated on you?'

'Something like that.' He forked up a piece of meat and gave a wry smile. 'Apparently I'm an object of fascination until I get married.'

'An eligible bachelor,' Jenny observed, pouring herself a glass of water.

'Water?' Alex mocked her gently, a smile playing around his firm mouth as he reached for the wine he'd uncorked. 'Don't you ever drink anything stronger than water?'

She smiled. 'Of course. But, to be honest, since Daisy was born I'm too exhausted to risk drinking. She wakes up quite often in the night and I need all the sleep I can get.'

He frowned slightly. 'It must have been very hard for you.' His voice was gruff. 'Tell me about Chloe.'

She stiffened slightly. 'Why do you want to know about Chloe?'

'Well, for a start because I'm being accused of corrupting her,' Alex said dryly. 'I think I at least deserve to know something about her.'

'I don't really think that you corrupted her. I do realise that it takes two…' Jenny pushed the food around her plate and then put her fork down. 'Chloe was very beautiful.'

'Describe her.'

Jenny hesitated. 'She was the sort of girl that made men do stupid things.' She gave an embarrassed smile. 'Long blonde hair like a mermaid, a figure with more curves than a country road.'

'Was she the reason you don't think you're attractive?'

Jenny looked at him warily. She'd never had this conversation with anyone before. And here she was having it with a man that she was supposed to loathe.

But the truth was she didn't loathe him, and he was an amazingly good listener.

'She was so beautiful that it was hardly surprising that men didn't pay me much attention when she was around,' she said lightly, picking up her water and taking a sip. 'It really didn't bother me. I loved her.'

'What was she like? Gentle, like you?'

Alex asked the question in the most direct fashion and she bit her lip.

'Chloe had a very difficult life. When Mum died she was only twelve, and Dad did everything he could to make it up to her. I think perhaps he overcompensated slightly.'

'You mean she was spoiled.'

'No!' Jenny denied it quickly and then bit her lip. 'Well, maybe, just a little, but it wasn't her fault. She was so young when Mum died.'

Alex frowned. 'You were young too, but he obviously didn't spoil you.'

'It was different for me.'

'Why?'

Jenny hesitated. 'Chloe was already quite…troubled.'

'Troubled?'

'A bit wild. Mixing with the wrong set. It started after Mum died. Dad tried his best but he couldn't really control her and his heart wasn't in it. He missed Mum too much. He died two years after she did.'

Alex pulled a face. 'You poor thing.'

'I was eighteen and already training to be a nurse but Chloe was living at home and she was hit really badly by it.' Jenny bit her lip. 'I switched hospitals so that I could live at home with her but I just couldn't get through to her. She stopped studying, fell in with a crowd who did nothing but party and after that—'

She broke off and he waited, his eyes on her face. 'After that, what?'

'She just seemed to go off the rails,' Jenny mumbled. 'I never knew where she was or who she was with. Sometimes she'd stay out all night without phoning. I'd wait up, worried sick. There were some nights when I didn't go to bed at all.'

'But you weren't her mother.'

Jenny gave a sad smile. 'That's exactly what Chloe said. After our parents died I did my best to keep everything together but I was pretty useless.' Her voice cracked slightly and she cleared her throat. 'Anyway, you don't want to hear all this.'

'I do want to hear it,' he said softly. 'It involves me, too, remember?'

It was the nearest he'd come to admitting that he'd had a relationship with her sister.

Jenny put her fork down. 'Eventually Chloe got fed up with me.' She gave him a brave smile. 'She said I was always breathing down her neck and I suppose I was. So she moved out of the house and lived with a group of friends. I hardly ever saw her after that. Every time I went round there she always seemed to be out and she never rang. It was purely by chance that I found out that she was pregnant.'

He gave a wry smile. 'And knowing you, I'm sure you were horrified.'

'Of course!' Jenny shot him an appalled look. 'She was only nineteen and really young for her age. And I know she was frightened, although she'd never admit it.'

'Did she tell you anything about the father?'

Jenny hesitated. 'All she'd say at first was that it was someone famous. She boasted that she was going to—' She broke off and closed her eyes briefly. She felt uncomfortable repeating her sister's words. 'Well, she said that she was going to—'

'Fleece him for money,' Alex finished, reaching for his glass. 'Don't be embarrassed to say it. When you have money there's always someone chasing after it. It's a fact of life.'

Jenny looked him in the eye. 'But that isn't why I'm here. Whatever Chloe had in mind, I'm not interested in your money.'

Suddenly it seemed really important that she convince him.

He looked at her thoughtfully. 'Strangely enough, I believe you. Anyway, carry on with the story.'

'Well, that's it really.' Jenny let out a breath. 'I tried to stay in touch but she avoided me as much as possible. I didn't even know she'd had the baby until the hospital rang to say she was very ill. Obviously she'd given me as next of kin. I dashed there as fast as I could. It was a nightmare.'

'And that's when she named me.' Alex leaned back in his chair, his face expressionless.

'Yes.'

'So why didn't you come and find me straight away?'

Jenny licked her lips. 'I was totally shattered by her death. I blamed myself for months. You know what it's like when someone dies—there's always guilt. And for me the guilt was that I'd allowed her to go through her pregnancy without me.'

Alex frowned. 'But she cut you out.'

'I know, but grief isn't rational,' Jenny muttered, taking a sip of her water. 'I felt I should have been there anyway, and as for coming to find you...' She broke off and he lifted an eyebrow.

'What?'

'I was angry with you,' she said simply. 'I thought you'd seduced her and abandoned her. Every paper I opened seemed to have a picture of you with a different girl in it.'

'Lots of those pictures are perfectly innocent,' Alex pointed out mildly, 'but the general public seem to be inordinately interested in my love life so the press print anything they can lay their hands on. It sells papers.'

Jenny nodded slowly. Now that the anger had died slightly she was beginning to see just how badly the man was hounded by the press. 'How come they don't come to your house?'

He gave a wicked grin. 'Because I actually have a different address that I use from time to time just to distract them.'

'Oh. That's clever.' She smiled. 'Well, anyway, I struggled by myself for a while but our quality of life was non-existent because the rent was so high in London.'

Alex pulled a face. 'And you were just on a nurse's salary?'

Jenny smiled. 'It wasn't that bad, but I decided that I was short-changing Daisy. She only had me and she deserved more than that. So I decided to find you.'

Alex looked at her in silence and then shifted in his chair. 'I'm almost sure she isn't mine,' he said gruffly, 'but either way I'll help you.'

Jenny looked at him warily. 'Why would you do that if she isn't yours?'

'Because I'm a sucker for a woman in trouble,' he said lightly, draining his wineglass and placing it carefully back on the table. 'And you, Jenny Phillips, are most definitely a woman in trouble.'

Her eyes meshed with his and something in the way he looked at her made her stomach turn over. She tried to look away but she found herself trapped by the look in his blue eyes.

She might have gazed at him for ever if Daisy's cry hadn't broken the connection.

Startled out of a forbidden daydream that shocked her, she was on her feet in an instant, knocking over the chair in her haste to get away from him. 'I'd better check if she's OK,' she mumbled unsteadily, and he gave a soft laugh.

'Saved by the baby,' he drawled, and although she was careful not to look at him, she knew that he was still looking at *her*. She *felt* it. 'Better run, Little Red Riding Hood, before the wolf gets you.'

She knew he was teasing her and her eyes flew to his, expecting to see laughter there, but for once his expression

was deadly serious and she swallowed hard before she
backed out of the room.

Oh, help.

What exactly had happened back there?

What had she been thinking?

Appalled by the strength of her reaction to a man she
supposedly disapproved of, she lifted Daisy with shaking
hands and wondered whether perhaps it was time she
looked for a small flat for herself and Daisy.

Living with Alex was proving to be more unsettling than
she could possibly have imagined.

Work continued to be horribly busy and things weren't
helped by a flu bug that seemed to hit half the staff in the
hospital.

'This can't be happening. It's the middle of summer,'
Tina grumbled as she tried to allocate the staff for the
morning shift. 'We shouldn't have flu. I've got two nurses
off and the agency is so stretched it can't provide any
cover.'

Jenny wasn't in a position to offer to work extra shifts
because she had to be at home with Daisy, but she knew
that some of the nurses were putting in a vast amount of
overtime. And so were the doctors.

Alex was working punishing hours and for the next four
days he was hardly at home.

She was forced to concede that her first opinion of him
had been horribly skewed by the reports she'd read in the
press.

It might be true that he avoided commitment like a life-
threatening disease, but it was also true that he was an
amazingly skilled and dedicated doctor, something the
newspapers always failed to comment on.

Even when one of the consultants was on duty, it was
still Alex who was called upon to deal with the really difficult cases. And there was no shortage of difficult cases.

As if to confirm that observation, the ambulance hotline rang, disturbing her thoughts, and Tina rushed to pick it up.

As she replaced the phone, Jenny looked at her expectantly. 'Well?'

'Thirty-four-year-old woman, thirty-one weeks pregnant coming in.' Tina was already hurrying towards Resus. 'She was found at the bottom of the stairs. Give Alex a yell, will you? I'll bleep the obstetric team.'

By the time Jenny had located Alex, the ambulance had arrived.

'Her pulse has been very rapid and I can't find a blood pressure at all,' the paramedic muttered as they quickly transferred her to the trolley. He gave a quick handover to Alex, outlining the patient's physical state.

'Give her high-flow oxygen and I want her tilted to the side. Use a pillow or a wedge, but I don't want her lying flat because the weight of the baby will press on her major blood vessels.' Alex talked as he worked, checking the airway and feeling for a pulse again. 'Get her attached to a monitor and I want two lines in—one in either arm. Everyone remember we're dealing with two patients here. Move!'

The whole team was aware of the seriousness of the situation and they worked fast to stabilise the woman but her condition deteriorated.

Alex talked clearly and calmly to the patient, even though there was no evidence that she was even aware of them. 'You're going to be fine, Jilly. You're in hospital now and we're going to sort out this problem and make sure that your baby is OK.' He glanced at one of the other doctors. 'Take blood for group and cross-match, urea and electrolytes, and then give her some Haemaccel. She's bleeding from somewhere and we need to start replacing fluid. Get the rest of her clothes off so that we can assess her properly and call the radiographers so that we can do some X-rays.'

Jenny glanced at him. 'What about the baby?'

His eyes lifted to hers and she read the tension there. 'We'll keep the abdominal and pelvic X-rays to a minimum and she can wear lead abdominal shields for the rest. Not ideal, I know, but I have to find out what's going on. 'Where the hell is the obs team? Did you call them, Tina?'

'They were in Theatre but they're coming as fast as they can.'

'Well, it's not fast enough,' Alex growled. 'Phone the ward and get a midwife down here with a CTG machine. I want the baby monitored. And someone get a Caesarean section pack ready. Just in case.'

Jenny exchanged stunned glances with Tina. Was he really contemplating doing a Caesarean section in A and E?

Despite the tension, everyone worked quickly and calmly and Alex was examining the first set of X-rays when the special registrar sucked in a breath.

'She's arrested,' he said, and Alex was back by her side in an instant.

'I need to intubate her.'

Jenny calmly handed him the laryngoscope and adjusted the light above his head.

'ET tube,' he snapped, but it was in his hand before he'd finished his brief order and Jenny found herself holding her breath as he attempted to intubate the patient.

She knew that inserting a tube into a patient's lungs was even harder when she was pregnant but fortunately Alex completed the procedure with no apparent difficulty and proceeded to ventilate the patient while the SR performed cardiac massage.

'Tom…' He turned to the SHO who'd inserted both the lines. 'I need you to take over here.'

The more junior doctor did as he was instructed and Alex strode over to the sink and started scrubbing. 'Open that

GET FREE BOOKS
and a
FREE GIFT WHEN YOU PLAY THE...

LAS VEGAS GAME

Just scratch off the gold box with a coin. Then check below to see the gifts you get!

YES!
I have scratched off the gold box. Please send me my **4 FREE BOOKS** and **gift for which I qualify.** I understand that I am under no obligation to purchase any books as explained on the back of this card. I am over 18 years of age.

M4EI

Mrs/Miss/Ms/Mr   Initials

BLOCK CAPITALS PLEASE

Surname

Address

Postcode

| 7 | 7 | 7 | **Worth FOUR FREE BOOKS plus a BONUS Gift!** |

Worth FOUR FREE BOOKS!

TRY AGAIN!

Visit us online at
www.millsandboon.co.uk

THE READER SERVICE™
FREE BOOK OFFER
FREEPOST CN81
CROYDON
CR9 3WZ

NO STAMP
NECESSARY
IF POSTED IN
THE U.K. OR N.I.

If offer card is missing write to: The Reader Service, PO Box 236, Croydon, CR9 3RU

Caesarean section pack and someone bleep the obstetricians again.'

Tina gaped at him. 'You're doing a Caesarean in here?'

'The baby is now in a hypoxic environment,' Alex reminded her roughly, lifting his forearms so that the soapy water ran down into the sink. 'We need to get it out of there if there's to be any hope that it'll survive. And getting the baby out will take the pressure off her inferior vena cava and improve the mother's blood supply so it might help her as well. Is anyone with her?'

Tina nodded. 'Her partner's in the relatives' room. He's really worried.'

'With good reason.' Alex's mouth was set in a grim line and he glanced up as one of the A and E consultants walked in. 'Mark! I need to do an emergency section—can you go and talk to the husband?'

They had a brief conversation, during which Alex slipped his arms into the gown that Jenny had carefully opened and snapped on a pair of sterile gloves.

In the meantime, one of the midwives from the obstetric unit had appeared and scrubbed up, ready to assist.

'Whatever you do, don't stop CPR,' Alex ordered, nodding with relief as the anaesthetist hurried into the room. 'Great. You can take over at the head end. Hurry up. I want to start. What's the foetal heart rate?'

The midwife checked. '105.'

'We need to get that baby out fast.' Alex cleaned the skin while the scrub nurse laid drapes over the woman. 'I'm starting.'

The anaesthetist nodded to indicate that he was ready and Alex picked up the scalpel and made an incision, his movements sure and confident.

Jenny watched in stunned amazement as he cut through layers of skin and muscle with such speed that she could barely keep up with what was happening.

In no time at all he was lifting the baby out, holding it head down and below the level of the mother's abdomen.

Somewhere in the course of the drama the paediatric and obstetric teams had arrived but seeing Alex confidently performing the emergency operation no one had interfered.

But now the baby had been delivered, they moved into action, taking the infant so that Alex could clamp and cut the cord.

The paediatricians took the baby away for assessment and Alex turned his attention back to the mother.

The atmosphere was tense and Jenny held her breath as she watched Alex work.

Would he be able to save the woman or would this be another little baby that ended up losing its mother?

Visions of Chloe, blonde-haired and laughing, flashed into her head and she swallowed down a lump in her throat.

Chloe shouldn't have died. She'd been so young.

Life was so unfair.

Oblivious to her distress, Alex was still concentrating on the mother. 'Here's the problem,' he said finally, gently removing the placenta from the uterus. 'Her placenta has started to come away. We need to give her some blood.'

'The lab just called with her results,' Jenny told him quickly, pushing aside the painful memories, 'so we've ordered some blood from the blood bank. It should be here any minute.'

'Right.' Alex glanced towards Hugo, the obstetric consultant. 'Over to you to close, if you don't mind. I want to try and sort the rest of her out.'

Hugo gave a wry smile. 'That was a pretty impressive section. I used to think I was fast until I saw that. Remind me never to travel in a car with you, if that's the speed you do everything.'

Alex smiled but he was already ripping off his gloves and turning his attention back to the patient, his eyes flickering to the monitors that gave him vital clues as to her condition.

There was a sudden wail from the corner of the room and Jenny gave a silent prayer of thanks.

The baby was crying.

Alex glanced up sharply. 'Is he OK?'

The paediatrician nodded. 'Seems to be. Bit on the small side, of course. Probably going to need a bit of help with his breathing but he's pretty good on the whole.'

Hugo glanced up from closing the uterus. 'Good job, Westerling. A few more minutes and that baby would have been dead. For a wealthy playboy you don't do half badly.'

But underneath the humour there was respect in his tone and Jenny bit her lip, realising that Alex had saved the baby's life.

But Alex wasn't listening to the praise being heaped on his head, he was concentrating on the mother, refusing to give up. Having saved the baby, he was obviously equally determined to save the mother.

'She's in sinus rhythm.' The anaesthetist glanced at Alex in amazement. He grinned like a little boy.

'Good work.'

Only when he was totally satisfied that the woman was stable did Alex sanction Jilly's transfer to the intensive care unit.

Mark strolled back into the room just as everyone was preparing for the transfer.

'She's doing all right?' There was no hiding the surprise in his voice and Alex gave a brief nod.

'For now. But we'll have to see how she goes.'

Mark looked stunned. 'And the baby?'

'The baby is on special care,' Tina told him, reaching up to hug Alex. 'And you are a clever man.'

'God's gift to women, that's me,' Alex drawled lightly, gently disengaging himself, 'especially pregnant ones.'

'Will you talk to her husband?'

Alex gave a nod. 'I'll do it now. We have no idea how she'll do in the long term, of course, but I'll discuss it with him.'

Jenny looked at him. 'Do you want me to come?'

'Yes.' He gave a nod and led the way out of the room. 'You're better at the emotional stuff than me. Are you OK? You look a bit pale.' His blue gaze was disturbingly acute. 'Were you thinking about Chloe?'

For a man who didn't think he was good at emotional stuff, he was amazingly intuitive. 'Yes.' She gave him a brave smile. 'Life's hard, isn't it?'

Alex nodded and lifted a hand to squeeze her shoulder. 'I'm sorry about your sister.'

Jenny swallowed, feeling his strength through the thin fabric of her uniform. 'Thanks. Oh, and by the way, I think you're fine with the emotional stuff,' she said softly, remembering just how hard he'd worked to save the mother and the baby. There hadn't been a man who didn't care. 'Except when it's about you.'

He paused outside the door, a wry smile playing around his firm mouth. 'More psychology? Don't push your luck, Red Riding Hood.'

His masculine voice was silky smooth and she caught her breath.

'You always keep yourself at a distance.'

His smile widened and he flipped her cheek casually with one lean finger. 'I can assure you that I don't.'

She coloured. 'I meant emotionally. And you're teasing me again.'

'I know.' His blue eyes glittered. 'But teasing you is such fun. It's fast becoming my favourite pastime.'

Without giving her a chance to answer, he pushed open the door and held it open so that she could walk through.

Later that evening they relaxed on the deck, eating a light supper while they enjoyed a spectacular sunset.

'Had you done one before?' Jenny couldn't forget the dramatic events of the day.

'Had I done what before?' Alex yawned and twisted some pasta around his fork.

'A Caesarean section.' Jenny wasn't really eating. She was still too wound up. 'You had that baby out in minutes.'

Alex shrugged. 'It was an emergency and, yes, to answer your question, I had done one before. Several, in fact.'

She looked at him curiously. 'You did obstetrics?'

'For a year. Why?'

'Because you just don't seem like the type of guy who'd enjoy it. All that emotion and children and you don't even like—' She broke off and he let out a long breath.

'I like children, Jenny,' he said quietly. 'I just don't want any of my own because I know I'd make a lousy father. And in a way you're right. Obstetrics didn't suit me. I did it because for a while I considered doing a GP rotation, but then I discovered that I missed A and E so I went back to that. But obviously I learned some skills along the way.'

'Like how to do the fastest section on record.'

Alex shrugged. 'Well, speed isn't always the most important factor, of course. For a routine section it's better to take more time, but in Jilly's case it was literally a matter of life or death so you take your chances and go with speed.'

'A sort of Ferrari version of a Caesarean section.' Jenny laughed and he smiled back, his eyes glittering dangerously.

'And just what do you know about Ferraris, Little Red Riding Hood?'

'Only that they're fast.' Her smile faded. 'Do you think they'll both be all right?'

Alex shrugged and pushed his plate away. 'Who knows? We did our best. Now we have to wait and see. The baby's still small but he should be OK.'

Jenny stared at him, blushing slightly. 'You were amazing.'

He lifted an eyebrow mockingly. 'I thought I was a rich playboy with wicked habits?'

Her blush deepened. 'You do have wicked habits but you were still amazing. You're a good doctor. And I don't think you'd make a lousy father at all. I think you'd be a very good father.'

He leaned back in his chair, his face inscrutable. 'That's not true.'

'Who has made you think otherwise?' It was almost an exact replica of the conversation they'd had about her appearance and his wry smile told her that he was aware of it.

'Trying to get smart, Red Riding Hood?'

'I just think the problem is in your head,' she said daringly, reminding him of his words to her, and he leaned forward, his gaze locked on hers.

'The problem,' he said slowly, 'is that I like my selfish, bachelor existence.'

'But you'd still make a good father.'

And with that she stood up quickly and picked up the plates, hurrying out of the room before he could reply.

CHAPTER SIX

TWENTY-FOUR hours after giving birth Jilly was well enough to be transferred to the maternity ward and everyone was hailing her recovery as a miracle.

'Which is a load of nonsense,' Tina said briskly as they prepared for another busy day. 'The only miracle around here was Alex Westerling.'

Jenny had to agree. 'I'll never forget how quickly he delivered that baby. I didn't even know he knew about babies.'

'Alex knows about everything,' Tina said dryly. 'He's a fantastic doctor but the press usually ignore that side of him. And he keeps it very quiet.'

And indeed Alex seemed almost embarrassed by all the fuss. When his skills weren't needed in Resus he spent most of the day in his office, wrestling with a report on staffing.

It was towards the end of the day that Jenny noticed that he didn't seem his usual self.

He looked flushed and there were lines of tiredness around his blue eyes.

She handed him some X-rays to check, her expression concerned. 'Are you all right?'

He stared at the X-ray. 'I'm fine.'

He didn't look fine.

He looked terrible and Jenny wondered whether he'd caught the flu bug that was going round.

Hopefully not, because without Alex she had a distinct feeling that the department would fall apart. He gave a great deal of himself to the hospital.

One look at him when they arrived home told her that she was right.

'I think you'd better go straight to bed,' she said gently, and he shot her a mocking glance that showed he'd lost none of his faculties.

'Propositioning me again, Miss Phillips?'

She gave him a placid smile. 'You're too ill to be a threat to my virtue, Dr Westerling.'

'Don't count on it, Red Riding Hood,' he said, but his voice rasped and his cheeks were flushed.

'Do you want supper?'

He shook his head and frowned slightly, lifting a hand to his head as if he were suddenly dizzy.

'No.' His jaw hardened and she sensed that for a man as strong and in control as Alex, being ill must be incredibly hard to cope with. 'I'm fine.'

She wished he'd stop saying that when he was clearly anything but fine!

She watched him drag himself up the stairs towards his room and let out a sigh. He most certainly was not fine but it was obvious that he wasn't going to reveal anything remotely like weakness to her.

Resolving to check on him later, she walked into the kitchen, made herself a salad and then curled up on one of his sofas with a book.

It was wonderfully peaceful after the hectic pace of the day and she was soon absorbed by the story, pausing only to sip the coffee she'd made herself.

She read until her eyelids started to ache and then closed the book and made her way to bed, checking on Daisy on the way. The baby was fast asleep, curled up in a ball on her tummy.

Jenny used the bathroom, changed into the T-shirt she wore to bed and went to check on Alex.

He was probably fast asleep, but still…

She padded along the landing and gently pushed open his bedroom door, frowning as she saw him sprawled over the bed, still fully clothed.

He was flushed and restless and she could see immediately that he had a high temperature.

Suddenly anxious, she hurried across to him and touched his forehead.

He was burning hot and he definitely shouldn't be wearing all those clothes.

'Alex...' She spoke gently but there was no response and she bit her lip.

She needed to get him undressed and into bed where at least he'd be more comfortable.

Deciding to start from the bottom and work upwards, she removed his shoes and then moved upwards to the button on his trousers. Her fingers shook slightly as she undid the button and slid his zip down.

Now all she had to do was remove his trousers.

Hoping desperately that he wouldn't wake up while she was doing it, she pulled the trousers gently over his hips, tugging harder as the fabric became stuck.

He gave a groan and his eyes flew open, his feverish gaze burning into hers.

'What are you doing?' His words slurred together and he moaned in protest as she finally removed his trousers and tried to shift him into the bed.

She hoped he didn't realise what she was doing. She could just imagine his comments if he woke up properly and realised that she was removing his trousers.

'You've fallen asleep with your clothes on. You need to get into bed, Alex.'

She tried to move him again but he was over six feet of powerfully built male and she didn't stand a chance of shifting him without some help.

'Alex—' she tried again '—can you move a bit—?'

He grunted and his eyes drifted shut again but he moved further onto the bed and she was able to yank the duvet out from under him and settle him against the pillows.

Having undressed him down to his pair of black silk

boxer shorts, she decided that enough was enough and went back onto the landing to find a fresh sheet. The last thing he needed was a duvet.

She tucked the sheet around him, checked his temperature again and then went back to her own room, carefully leaving the door open so that she could hear him if he needed her.

Alex was ill for three days, his temperature so high that Jenny called the doctor twice because she was so worried.

The doctor told her impatiently that it was just flu and that all she could do was make him as comfortable as possible. So she did that, even though he hardly seemed to know that she was there.

He was so hot that twice she changed the sheets, struggling to shift his powerful body enough to enable her to remake the bed.

It was fortunate that she had four days off and that Daisy was relatively content just to play in the upstairs rooms. In the end Jenny gave up on her own room and camped out in Alex's bedroom, nursing him night and day, wishing desperately that he'd get better.

The doctor had assured her that his temperature would come down but there was no sign of it and she sponged him regularly, trying to make him more comfortable even though he didn't even seem to know she was there.

The nights were the worst, sitting there, trying to calm him down as he shivered and muttered incomprehensibly under his breath, totally unaware of her presence.

On the evening of the third day she was so worried about him that she curled up at the bottom of his bed so that she could doze but still be aware of any change in him. She'd already resolved to call the doctor again in the morning if there was no change. She didn't care how irritated he was with her. She wanted him to check Alex again. She was due back at work but there was no way she could go. Alex needed her.

'Jenny—Jen...' His hoarse voice woke her and she propped herself up on her elbows, muzzy-headed from sleep.

It was the first time he'd said her name since he'd become ill and she let out a sigh of relief.

He was better. He must be better.

She'd left a small light turned on so that she could see him in the night, and without thinking she crawled up the bed and touched her face to his cheek, noting that it was cooler.

'Oh, thank goodness.' She sank back on her heels, her slim shoulders sagging with relief. 'You had me worried for a while there.'

Very worried.

'I feel terrible.' His jaw was darkened with three days' worth of stubble and his hair was tousled but somehow he still managed to look dangerously handsome.

It occurred to her that for the past three days she hadn't thought of him as a man but as someone who needed nursing.

Now that the worst had passed she realised with appalling clarity that he was very much a man and she was kneeling on his bed in front of him, wearing nothing more than a skimpy T-shirt that only just covered her bottom.

Hopefully he wouldn't be able to see much in the dimly lit bedroom.

'Of course you feel terrible. You've been really, really ill.' She tried to slide away from him, scarlet with mortification, but long fingers curled around her wrist, preventing her escape.

'Don't go.' His voice was scratchy and she glanced at him, feeling hideously self-conscious.

She was half-naked, for goodness' sake!

'I'll just get some clothes on and I'll be back.' She tugged at her wrist again but his grip merely tightened.

'You didn't seem to care about what you were wearing when you thought I was asleep,' he pointed out, and she flushed.

'Well, of course I didn't. I was worried about you. You've been very ill.'

His gaze was curiously intent. 'And you looked after me.' His dark brows came together as he obviously searched his mind for some memory of the past few days. 'What the hell happened?'

He sounded so much like the old Alex that she smiled with relief, forgetting for a moment that she was still kneeling on the bed with his long fingers clamped round her wrist.

'You caught flu, that's what happened. And you caught it badly. I've had the doctor out twice. Your doctor hates me, by the way.'

He looked at her blankly. 'The doctor?'

'That's right,' she said lightly. 'One of those creatures who think they know everything.'

His eyes narrowed as he studied her closely. 'You don't look too great yourself.'

'Thank you.'

'I mean you look exhausted. You've got dark circles under your eyes. Did I keep you awake?'

For three whole days and nights.

'Just a bit,' she hedged, wishing that he'd stop looking at her. Being the focus of his attention was decidedly unsettling, 'But now you're better I'll go back to my room.'

'Not yet.' He showed no signs of releasing her and she chewed her lip, horribly conscious of the short T-shirt. It only just reached the tops of her thighs. 'Was I a terrible patient?'

She shook her head. 'Surprisingly not.' She gave a wry smile. 'You're easier to handle asleep than awake.'

Despite the fact that he was obviously still feeling rough, his eyes gleamed. 'Is that so?'

She was suddenly achingly aware of the breadth of his shoulders, of the nest of dark hair on his chest and the fact that he was wearing virtually nothing. She knew that for sure. After all, she'd been the one who'd undressed him.

She was desperate to escape from the room and dress in something more appropriate. 'Would you like a drink or something to eat?'

He shook his head. 'What I do need is a visit to the bathroom.' He grimaced and shifted in the bed, 'How have I been managing that?'

She flushed scarlet and tugged her wrist away from his grip. 'I've been helping you.'

'Have you now?' He gave a humourless laugh. 'It's a good job you're not romantically attached to me, isn't it? I'm sure helping me to the bathroom would have killed any relationship stone dead.'

'That's because you associate relationships with sex and not caring,' she said quietly, and he cast her an odd look.

'Do I?'

'Yes. You only do the physical stuff, not the emotional stuff. But we're not going to talk about your deficiencies in that area now. Do you want to use the bathroom or not?'

For a moment he appeared to be speechless and then he coughed and winced slightly. 'I'll give it a try on my own.'

She couldn't resist teasing him. 'You don't need to be shy. I'm fairly well acquainted with your body, having sponged it with tepid water for the past three days.'

'So why are you dying to escape?' he drawled, and her smile faded. Even in his weakened state he was devastatingly attractive.

'Because the wolf has woken up,' she muttered, backing towards the door, wishing that she hadn't teased him. Teasing Alex was playing with fire. Even when he was ill he was lethally attractive and mentally alert.

He stood up and immediately staggered. She was back by his side in an instant, concern for him overwhelming any shyness that she felt. She took his arm so that he could lean on her.

'You're not well enough to be out of bed without help,' she scolded, helping him towards the bathroom, trying not to notice as he slid an arm round her shoulders.

He was just using her for support, she reminded herself firmly, escorting him as far as the bathroom.

'There we are—you can manage this bit by yourself. I'll go and get you a drink. I'll be back in a minute.'

When she'd had time to dress in something more appropriate and remind herself that Alex Westerling was absolutely not her type.

Alex lay in bed watching as Jenny straightened the sheets and replenished his drink. She was a born nurturer, he reflected. A woman who was never happier than when she was taking care of people. You only had to look at the way that she cared for Daisy to see that. And the child wasn't even hers.

And now he was on the receiving end of that warmth and it felt good. Better than he ever would have imagined.

He couldn't remember ever being cared for like this before, not even as a child.

Her hands were unbelievably gentle, her voice warm and soothing, and just having her there made him feel a hundred times better.

She was peaceful and soothing and calmed the atmosphere more effectively than the scented candles she'd insisted on placing in his room.

She'd dragged on a dressing-gown that covered her from neck to ankle but she may as well not have bothered. He had a very vivid memory of a pair of sensational long legs that had been the first thing he'd seen when he'd opened his eyes.

He'd pretended not to notice because she'd clearly been embarrassed by her lack of attire, but he was incredibly touched by the fact that she'd been sleeping at the bottom of his bed. She must have been seriously worried about him.

And she obviously hadn't had much sleep herself. She looked done in.

'How the hell did you cope, looking after Daisy as well as me?'

She smiled. 'You were much more demanding than Daisy. She's a very easy baby. I put her on the mat on the floor and she played happily. At night she slept.'

But Jenny had been awake all night looking after him. And then all day looking after Daisy. No wonder she looked so exhausted.

The fact that she'd made such a sacrifice for someone she disapproved of as thoroughly as him made him feel vaguely uncomfortable.

He shifted slightly in the bed but the feeling remained and he realised that it wasn't physical.

She placed a hand on his forehead and frowned anxiously. 'How are you feeling now?'

'Pretty weak.'

It was true, but he also knew that in normal circumstances he would have died rather than admit weakness to a woman. But he'd discovered that there was no nicer feeling than being cared for by Jenny. And he liked the fact that she no longer seemed so wary of him.

Not that he could have done anything remotely shock-inducing if he'd wanted to, he reflected wryly. He was too weak to pounce on anyone, even someone as slightly built as Jenny.

Alex's eyes followed her as she tidied up the room, noticing the long, sooty lashes and the fullness of her lower lip. Even the bulk of the dressing-gown couldn't disguise her slender, feminine body. She was incredibly beautiful, he decided, especially now when she didn't know that he was watching her. He struggled with an impulse to drag the dressing-gown off and discover if the rest of her was as good as her legs.

She finished tidying and glanced at him. 'You should get some sleep,' she said softly. 'I'll leave the door open so that you can call if you need me.'

He felt a pang of disappointment that she was no longer going to sleep on the end of his bed. And then he realised that what he really wanted was for her to sleep *in* the bed.

With him.

He closed his eyes and clenched his jaw. What the hell was the matter with him?

Jenny wasn't his type.

Not because she wasn't blonde but because she wasn't the sort of woman that played by his rules. Jenny didn't even know how to flirt. In fact, he wouldn't be surprised if she was still a virgin. Something had to explain why she always looked so shocked and uncomfortable whenever the subject of his sex life was raised.

She disapproved heartily of his wicked ways and the sooner he booted her out of his house, the safer for her.

And him.

Alex returned to work three days later despite Jenny's strenuous attempts to persuade him to stay at home.

'You've been really ill,' she protested as they ate breakfast together, and he shot her that impatient look that she was getting to know so well.

'You're being wifely again.'

She bit her lip. 'I just don't think you're ready to go back to work.'

'If I collapse you can resuscitate me,' he promised, flashing her a wicked smile that made her catch her breath. She couldn't stop her eyes drifting down to his mouth.

What would it be like to be kissed by Alex?

Exciting…

'Stop looking at me like that, Red Riding Hood,' he said hoarsely, the expression in his sharp blue eyes telling her that he knew exactly what she'd been thinking. He drained his coffee and put the mug down on the table with a thump. 'Let's get out of here before we both do something we'll regret.'

This time she didn't argue.

She'd never been so confused in her life. This was the man who treated women with a carelessness that appalled her. He went through life avoiding any sort of commitment. He was totally wrong for her.

So why was she suddenly noticing every small thing about him? Like the way he teased old ladies and showed the utmost patience with people who were frightened and in pain? And the way he waded in confidently, determined to do his utmost to save a mother and her unborn child? And the way his cheeks creased when he smiled and the way he always seemed to have the beginnings of stubble on his hard jaw? Why did she suddenly want to run her fingers through that glossy black hair, just to see how it felt?

But he wasn't hers to touch, she reminded herself, feeling suddenly helpless under the pull of emotions she'd never experienced before.

In fact, he wasn't anybody's.

Alex was a loner. A man who kept himself at a safe emotional distance from everyone around him.

And he wasn't going to make an exception for a small dark-haired girl with a flat chest, who worried about his drinking habits and had never even had a proper boyfriend.

Pulling herself together, Jenny fastened Daisy into her car seat and drove to work, trying to think about anything other than Alexander Westerling.

Fortunately work was so busy that she had absolutely no chance to dwell on her confusing response to him.

From the minute she arrived on the unit she was working flat out, and as the day progressed she wondered how Alex was coping. She knew that he must still be feeling rough.

'I need you in Resus, Jenny,' Tina said briskly, her face drawn and tired. She'd been coping with a staffing crisis for more than a week and it was beginning to show. 'They're bringing in a 64-year-old man who collapsed in a shopping centre.'

The ambulance arrived before she finished her sentence and the man was hurried into Resus.

Jenny glanced up with relief as Alex strode into the room. He looked grim-faced and pale but he applied himself with the same ruthless efficiency as ever.

'What have we got?'

'This is Geoffrey Palmer…' The paramedics handed over quickly and Jenny carefully placed an oxygen mask over the man's face lifting it slightly as he gestured to talk.

He looked at her with frightened eyes. 'What's happening?'

'We're going to find that out now,' Jenny said firmly, her voice steady and her eyes sympathetic as she checked his pulse and blood pressure.

Alex was already examining the man, his gaze flickering briefly to Tom who'd accompanied him into Resus. 'Two lines in, please. Large-bore cannulae.'

Tom nodded and reached for the equipment while Alex continued his examination.

'I want him on a monitor, Jenny. Mr Palmer, can you describe the pain for me?'

The man groaned. 'Round my stomach and my back…'

'We'll give you something for the pain right now.' Alex quickly undid the buttons of the man's shirt to give him access to the abdomen.

Tom moved away from the trolley. 'Two lines are in.'

'Give him some morphine for the pain and cyclizine and then take blood for FBC, U and Es, glucose, base-line co-

agulation screen, LFTs and emergency cross-matching.'
Alex listed the investigations he wanted and then paused
briefly, his eyes on the more junior doctor. 'And I want ten
units of red cells and two units of platelets.'

Tom stared at him and then gave a brief nod as he
reached for the necessary blood bottles.

Jenny bit her lip and concentrated on the patient. It was
obvious from the volume of blood that Alex had ordered
that he thought that the patient was at risk of a major bleed.

'Jenny, can you fast-bleep the vascular surgeon, the on-
call anaesthetist and warn Emergency Theatre?' Alex finished examining the patient's abdomen and Jenny noticed
that the patient's skin was mottled over his lower body.

Alex was staring at the monitor. 'He's tachycardic and
hypotensive. Tom, give him a unit of Haemaccel.' He
turned his attention back to the patient and put a reassuring
hand on the man's shoulder. 'Mr Palmer, we need to pass
a tube into your bladder and then you're going to need an
operation I'm afraid.'

The man groaned. 'What's happening to me?'

'You have what we call an aortic aneurysm,' Alex said
briefly, looking up as a man hurried into the room dressed
in theatre scrubs. 'Paul—thanks for coming.'

He briefly outlined the condition of the patient and the
vascular surgeon examined him and pronounced that he'd
operate immediately.

'I'll clear the corridors and get them to hold the lifts,'
Jenny said, knowing that the transfer to Theatre was crucial
and that any delay could be life-threatening.

She made the necessary calls, checked the oxygen and
suction and made sure that all the right equipment was
ready for the short trip to Theatre.

If anything happened on the way, they needed to be prepared.

'Mr Palmer, is there anyone you'd like me to call?' she
asked, and the man nodded, his face pale and sweaty.

'My daughter. Can you phone my daughter? She works on Anderson Ward.'

Jenny made a note of the name and handed it to one of the other staff nurses who promised to call straight away.

Fortunately the transfer passed without incident and the patient was wheeled into Theatre within minutes.

Jenny hurried back to A and E and made her way to Resus to clear and restock the room.

Tom and Alex were still there, deep in conversation.

Tom raked his fingers through his hair, visibly stressed. 'But how did you know it was an aortic aneurysm? You knew straight away.'

'He had classic symptoms.'

Tom pulled a face. 'Well, you gave me a fright when you ordered all those units of blood.'

'My guess is he's going to need every one of them. If that aneurysm bursts, he's going to have a massive bleed,' Alex said grimly, his handsome face pale and drawn. 'We were lucky to get him to Theatre.'

Jenny looked at him, hiding her concern.

She knew he wouldn't thank her for it, but she was worried about him.

There was absolutely no doubt in her mind that he should have been at home, resting, not working a punishing schedule in the A and E department.

She was desperate to persuade him to go home but she knew there was no point. Alex would do exactly what he wanted to do.

All she could do was finish her shift, go home and hope that he wasn't in too bad a state when he finally appeared.

CHAPTER SEVEN

HE FELT terrible.

It was almost nine when Alex eventually arrived home and the first thing that hit him as he walked into the house was a delicious smell coming from the kitchen.

He closed his eyes briefly and gave a wry smile.

He was rapidly adjusting to having a woman in the house. There was something amazingly restful about coming home to Jenny's cooking.

She walked out of the kitchen, her green eyes anxious, and he realised with profound shock that it wasn't coming home to her cooking that was restful, it was coming home to Jenny.

It was the patient syndrome, he told himself firmly. He was fixated on his nurse.

Goodness only knew what a psychiatrist would make of that.

'You look awful.' She frowned at him in concern. 'You never should have stayed so long.' She touched his arm gently in a gesture of sympathy and he felt his body harden in response to her touch.

Suddenly all he wanted was to drag her off to bed and rediscover those incredibly long legs.

Damn.

This was getting really bad.

The sooner his lawyer called the better for both of them.

'Where's Daisy?'

'Fast asleep.'

So even the baby wasn't going to provide a distraction. Gritting his teeth, he disengaged himself from her and paced across the room to pour himself a drink.

He paused with his hand on the bottle and then glanced over his shoulder towards her with a sigh.

'Go on. Say it. I shouldn't be drinking.'

'You've had a lousy day, Alex,' she said quietly, her green eyes warm with sympathy. 'You're entitled to a drink if you want it.'

Suddenly he found that he didn't want it.

He could think of a much better way to relax.

But what he really wanted was totally off limits.

Jenny was staring at him in consternation and it occurred to him that if she could read his mind she'd run a mile.

In fact, she ought to be running a mile. He wasn't sure that he was safe around her any more.

He sucked in a breath and ran a hand over the back of his neck to relieve the tension. It was taking all his will-power not to drag her into his arms and it was getting to the stage where he didn't trust himself around her. Normally if he met a woman that he liked and she played by his rules then he was perfectly happy to pursue the relationship to its natural conclusion. Which was nearly always bed.

But Jenny was different.

Jenny didn't do bed.

Not in the casual sense, anyway.

She was looking at him with concern. 'Can I do anything? Would you like me to run you a bath or something?'

Despite the building tension, his eyes gleamed. 'Ah— we're back to the bath again.' Maybe if he teased her it would help. 'Jenny's answer to all of life's problems.'

He waited for her to blush, the way she always did when he teased her, but this time she smiled, her cheeks dimpling slightly.

'You should try it,' she suggested mildly. 'It works.'

'Only if you show me how.'

He was trying to shock her into backing off. Trying to warn her to run for cover while she still had the chance.

But she didn't run. Instead, she gave him that lovely smile that almost made him groan with longing.

'Don't be ridiculous, Alex,' she said mildly. 'I know you're joking.'

He wondered what she'd say if she knew he was deadly serious. At the present moment there was nothing he'd like more than to share a bath with Jenny.

She was totally unlike any woman he'd ever been involved with before, but maybe that was part of the attraction, he mused silently.

One thing was sure, she'd be hideously shocked if she could read his thoughts.

Hell, he was shocking himself.

'I'm going for a swim.' Hopefully the freezing water would dampen down some of those hormones of his that were raging out of control. 'I'm stiff after standing in one position for too long.'

She stared at him, appalled. 'Alex, you can't swim now! It's already dark.'

He shrugged carelessly. 'It's fine. I often do it.'

'Please, don't.' She bit her lip. 'I've had about as much trauma as I can stand for one week. You've only just got over a horrid bout of flu. You've been at work all day. If you get into trouble in the water…'

His tension increased and he moved his shoulders and grimaced. 'My shoulders are aching from standing in one place for so long.'

'Then lie down on the sofa and I'll give you a massage,' she suggested, and then rolled her eyes. 'I suppose you'll take that the wrong way, too.'

He gave a wry smile. 'You're becoming harder and harder to shock, Jenny Phillips. That's what comes of living with such a disreputable rake as me.'

Her eyes slid away from his. 'You're not so bad, but as you've brought the subject up…' She hesitated and cleared her throat. 'I have rung a couple of agents looking for a flat.'

He felt as though he'd been kicked in the stomach and then frowned. Hell, wasn't that exactly what he wanted? For Jenny to move out?

No.

It was the last thing he wanted. 'Why would you do that?'

She avoided his gaze. 'Because the issue of Daisy's paternity is taking longer to sort out than I thought it would. I—I truly hadn't intended to land myself on you indefinitely. Sooner or later Daisy and I are going to need somewhere of our own,' she said quietly, 'and obviously I want to stay near to you so that you can see Daisy.'

Was he bothering her as much as she was bothering him?

He narrowed his eyes and looked at her closely, searching for clues, but he couldn't tell much if she refused to look at him.

Unless that was a sign in itself.

'Why would you want to move out? You're struggling with money as it is and if you start paying rent…' He shook his head. 'No. Forget it. You and Daisy stay here until my lawyers come up with an answer on her paternity. Then we'll work out the best course of action.'

He didn't want her moving out.

He wanted her where he could keep an eye on her.

But before he could argue the point further, the pressures of the day finally caught up with him and he felt the room shift.

She noticed immediately. 'Go upstairs. Lie down on the bed and I'll bring you some supper.'

He didn't argue.

Instead, he dragged himself upstairs and sprawled on the bed, eyes closed, and moments later he heard her soft tread as she walked into the room.

He was still wondering whether he could be bothered to

get undressed when he felt the bed dip as she sat down beside him.

'Take your shirt off and roll over.'

He opened one eye and gave her a wry look. 'Is that your best pick-up line?'

'It's my massage line.' She reached out and undid the buttons on his shirt herself. For a moment he thought he saw her fingers tremble slightly but when he looked at her face she was perfectly calm and he decided that he must have imagined it. 'You take it off while I light the candles.'

'Candles?' He shrugged out of his shirt, noticing for the first time that she'd placed several candles next to the bed, along with some tiny bottles. 'Why do we need candles?'

'I'm trying to create the right atmosphere to help you relax.'

She lit the candles, flicked off the main lights and the bedroom was immediately plunged into semi-darkness, lit only by an intimate glow.

Relax?

Alex shot her an incredulous look and then realised that she truly had no idea what she was doing. He swore softly under his breath. She was unbelievably naïve about sex. Here she was with a half-naked man on the bed and she was lighting candles.

She obviously believed that she was creating an atmosphere of relaxation whereas, in fact, what she'd created was an atmosphere of seduction.

The dimly lit room, the scented oils and a half-naked man on the bed...

And he didn't feel relaxed at all.

In fact, his whole body was throbbing with suppressed sexual tension.

He propped himself up on his elbows and watched as she walked back into his bathroom and picked up some towels.

She spread one out on the bed next to him and then gave him a shy smile.

'You might want to take your trousers off. If you fall asleep you're going to be uncomfortable in them.'

Fall asleep? There was absolutely no way he'd fall asleep the way he felt at the moment, and as for the trousers—well, at least they were covering up his reaction to her.

Nevertheless he found himself undoing his trousers and sliding them down his thighs.

She was warming some oil between her hands. 'Now, lie on your front and I'll cover your lower half so you don't get cold.'

He gritted his teeth and did as he was told, although lying on his stomach wasn't easy given his current physical condition. At least it would make it easier to disguise how she made him feel.

He had a feeling that she didn't have a clue and he didn't want to embarrass her. He liked the fact that she seemed to have lost some of her wariness around him.

He closed his eyes and tried to think of something suitably neutral and boring, something that didn't involve being semi-naked while Jenny rubbed oil into his body.

Even so, the first touch of her hands on his skin made him groan and he knew that if her intention was to make him relax, she'd chosen the wrong activity. There was no way he would ever be able to relax while Jenny was sliding her palms over his shoulders in such a seductive fashion.

He never would have guessed that she had such good hands.

She hadn't seemed a particularly tactile person—at least, not with him.

But her hands slid over him in a smooth, seamless motion that ignited the most wicked of fantasies in his active mind. She had the most incredible touch.

The touch of a lover.

He lay still, his eyes closed as she worked on his shoulders and then moved slowly down his back.

She didn't speak and the silence merely intensified the erotic thoughts throbbing in his brain.

Her hands slid smoothly over his body, gliding lower, and he groaned again.

She paused. 'Am I hurting you?'

She really had no idea.

He decided enough was enough and rolled onto his back, his jaw tense and his eyes closed.

'I think you'd better stop.'

She frowned, puzzled. 'But—'

His eyes opened and what she read in them must have made an impact because she sucked in a breath.

'Run, Red Riding Hood,' he said softly, his gaze fixed on her face. 'Run while you still can.'

She froze then, her green eyes locked on his. But she didn't seem able to move. She reminded him of a delicate, gentle animal who has just realised that she's been playing with the ultimate predator.

Torn between fascination and terror.

He gritted his teeth and fought the very male impulse to grab her and roll her under him.

'Go, Jenny,' he said hoarsely. 'For heaven's sake, just go.'

She spoke then, her voice breathy and very feminine. 'I'm sorry if I did something wrong…'

Damn. She should be running to her room and locking the door behind her.

'You didn't do anything wrong.'

'But—'

She obviously had no idea of the danger she was in.

Swearing softly under his breath, he reached for her and pulled her down, rolling her under him as he'd been dying to do from the moment she'd lit the candles.

Or maybe from before that. He didn't know. All he knew

was that he wanted Jenny and that she wasn't running fast enough.

'You should have run, Red Riding Hood, while you had the chance.'

She stared up at him, her breath coming in little pants, her pupils dilated. 'I can't run...'

'Well, you should,' he growled, lifting a hand and pulling her hair out of the clip that she always wore. He combed his fingers through the silky strands of dark hair, deciding that he'd never felt anything so soft and smooth. 'Push me away, Jenny.'

His mouth hovered above hers and he could feel the warmth of her breath mingling with his.

'Stop me, Jenny.'

She stared up at him helplessly, enthralled and hypnotised by his burning gaze. 'I can't.'

His mouth brushed lightly against hers and he groaned as delicious sensation arced through his tense body. 'I'll hurt you.'

'You wouldn't.'

Her tongue flickered against his lips and Alex gave up all attempts at restraint.

He touched his mouth gently to hers, dipping his tongue inside, persuading her to open for him. And she did. His hand still locked in her hair, he kissed her deeply, tasting her sweetness, feeling her shuddering response against him.

Her tongue tangled with his and she kissed him back without restraint, kissed him until the blood throbbed in his veins and he felt as though his body might explode.

He knew he ought to lift his head to let them both breathe, but kissing Jenny was shockingly addictive and he couldn't bring himself to end it even for a moment.

His free hand slid downwards and heat flared inside him as he gently drew a thumb over one pebbled nipple. She gasped against his mouth and he repeated the movement and then slid his hand under her T-shirt, his whole body throbbing with the need to have her naked under him. He unclipped her bra without the slightest difficulty and then finally dragged his mouth away from hers.

She lay looking up at him, flushed and fevered from his kiss, her eyes totally trusting.

He knew he should stop.

He was going to stop.

And then she breathed in deeply and he heard the jerk in her breath and felt the brush of her nipple against his searching fingers.

Unable to help himself, Alex slid her T-shirt up, exposing her breasts to his hungry gaze.

She was small and delicate and utterly female, and the male in him struggled to control the powerful surge of desire that swamped his body.

Aware that he was torturing himself, he lowered his head and flicked at one dusky pink nipple with his tongue, groaning as it hardened under his skilled touch.

She gasped his name and clung to the muscles of his shoulders as if she was falling and he was the only one who could keep her safe.

But he wasn't going to keep her safe.

He was going to hurt her.

He always hurt women.

He lifted his head and gave a soft curse, fully intending to end the kiss while they both still could, but his eyes locked onto her nipple, glistening damply from his touch.

Her breathing was shallow and her hips writhed subtly against the sheets as she sought to relieve the incredible tension that was building inside both of them.

She was all softness and warmth and feminine temptation, her eyes and her body begging him for more, and Alex, who had never lost control of his reactions in his life before, suddenly lost control

He moved upwards again and brought his mouth down on hers, his free hand sliding lower until he found the hem of her skirt. He drew it upwards, feeling the warmth of her skin against the ends of his fingers, feeling the press of her sweet body as she arched against him. He shifted slightly to allow himself better access, his hand gliding smoothly up her inner thigh and brushing the damp silk of her panties.

His desire fuelled still further by this explicit evidence of her need for him, his fingers slid inside the elastic and gently touched the very heart of her.

Sensitive as he was to her every tremor, he felt her sudden tension and his hand stilled.

'Alex…' She croaked his name against his mouth and he lifted his head slightly, his breathing decidedly unsteady, his fingers still resting gently on the most private part of her.

'Do you want me to stop?'

'No—yes…' She closed her eyes and gave a whimper. 'I don't know. It's just that I've never—I haven't…'

She was a virgin.

And suddenly Alex found the willpower he'd been looking for.

He moved his hand and rolled away from her, closing his eyes as he struggled to calm his throbbing body.

There was a moment's silence while he fought to regain control—while he wrestled with his conscience.

'Alex?' She said his name, her voice barely a whisper, and he gave a sigh and opened his eyes.

'I told you to run.'

'But I didn't want to run.'

'Well, you should have done,' he said roughly, sitting up and sliding off the bed in a lithe movement. He needed to get away from him. Fast. 'I'm no good for you, Jenny. You know that. We should never have started this.'

'But—'

'Jenny, I'm everything you accused me of being the day you first turned up here with your accusing gaze and your innocent expression.' His voice was harsh. 'Nothing's changed.'

'That's not true. I didn't know you when I arrived. I said things—' She broke off and bit her lip. 'I said awful things about you, I know, but that was before I knew you.'

He gritted his teeth. 'Jenny, I'm everything you thought I was, sweetheart.'

She shook her head. 'You're a brilliant doctor. You give so much of yourself to others but you like to hide it. And you're wonderful with Daisy. You're going to be a great father.'

He raked long fingers through his tousled dark hair. 'Jenny, I will make a lousy father. I don't do relationships. You know that. I don't get close to people.'

She looked at him. 'Why?'

He recognised the look in her eyes and swore under his breath. She thought she could change him. She thought she'd be different from the others, but what she didn't realise was that the problem didn't lie with the other women he'd been with—the problem lay with *him*.

He just couldn't commit to anyone.

He didn't want to. And Jenny was no exception.

All he wanted was a brief, uncomplicated relationship.

'Because that's the way it is.' He saw the hurt in her eyes and cursed himself. Why the hell had he ever let it get this far?

Hating himself for what he had to do, he ran a hand over his face and looked at her.

'I don't sleep with women like you.'

'Because I'm not blonde?'

Her feeble attempt at a joke did nothing to relieve his tension. However had he got himself in this position? 'Because you don't do just sex, do you, Jenny? And that's all I'm offering.'

His blunt words made her flinch and she looked at him like a kitten that knew it was being sent away from its mother. 'I'm not a threat to you, Alex,' she said softly, and he gave a wry smile.

With her gentle warmth and her calm nature she was the biggest threat that he'd ever encountered.

And tomorrow he was putting serious pressure on his lawyer to find an answer to Daisy's paternity.

He wanted the issue settled so that he could get Jenny out of his life.

Before he did something that was going to hurt both of them.

Ending the conversation abruptly, he strode into the bathroom and locked the door, turned the shower full on and switched the setting to cold.

Jenny stared at the locked bathroom door, feeling totally numb.

He'd rejected her.

But that wasn't surprising, was it? How could she possibly compete with the women he usually mixed with?

And she'd totally blown it by reacting like a gauche schoolgirl. But his touch had been so overwhelmingly intimate and she'd been terrified by the power of her own response.

She slid off his bed, filled with embarrassment, wondering how on earth she was going to face the man in the morning.

It was all her fault. What on earth had possessed her to give him a massage? The minute he'd removed his shirt and exposed his smooth, well-muscled chest she'd realised the depth of her mistake but it had been too late to correct it without drawing attention to the sudden awareness that had engulfed her.

And to be fair to the man, he'd given her every opportunity to pull away.

But she hadn't been able to do so.

She'd been trapped by the chemistry that had pulsed between them, in the thrall of something far stronger than common sense.

All the warnings in the world wouldn't have stopped her from experiencing Alex's kiss.

Groaning at the memory, she slid back into her room and closed her eyes briefly.

What had she been thinking of?

Guilt stabbed her. This was the man that Chloe had loved. They'd made a child together.

How could she have forgotten that this was the man that broke Chloe's heart?

Because he wasn't the man she'd thought he was.

If he hadn't detected her lack of experience, where would they be now?

Making love…

Only it wasn't love, she reminded herself. It was sex and, as Alex had said, she didn't do sex.

Or did she?

She certainly never had before but she was painfully aware that if Alex hadn't exerted his awesome willpower to break off the physical contact she would have gone wherever he'd chosen to take her.

Jenny sat at the table in the kitchen, feeding Daisy, dreading Alex's arrival.

She'd thrown herself at her sister's lover and he'd had to tactfully reject her.

She ought to be grateful to him for saving them both from a huge mistake but at the moment she couldn't see past the humiliation of having thrown herself at a man who didn't want her.

Where on earth did they go from here?

But when Alex strode into the kitchen five minutes later he didn't show even a flicker of embarrassment.

But, then, he must be used to women flinging themselves

at him, she reflected miserably, concentrating her attention on Daisy as he poured himself coffee and pulled out a chair.

He sat down, stretched his long legs out in front of him and reached for a freshly baked roll.

She was making a determined effort not to look at him but she knew he was looking at her.

'Good morning.' His voice was soft and very male and connected with every female part of her.

How did he do that? she wondered helplessly, trying to stop her hand shaking as she lifted the spoon to Daisy's mouth. He was sitting on the other side of the table but already her heart was thumping and her pulse was racing. The moment Alex entered a room it seemed to throb with sexual tension.

'Good morning.' She answered without looking at him and there was a brief silence.

'You're going to have to look at me some time, Red Riding Hood,' he murmured finally, a touch of amusement in his velvety tones. 'It was just a kiss, sweetheart. There's no need to be shy.'

Just?

The man obviously had no idea just how well he kissed.

But the fact that he could dismiss it so easily just confirmed her belief that it had meant absolutely nothing to him. She already knew that, of course. He'd been the one who'd ended it. And she'd virtually begged him not to…

Embarrassment swamped her again and she wished he'd go to work and leave her alone.

But he obviously wasn't going anywhere.

Instead, he poured himself some more coffee and her eyes slid to his hands, fixing on the dark hairs just visible below the cuffs of his shirt. Everything about Alex was sexy. Even his hands. *The same hands that had touched her so skilfully the night before.*

She dragged her attention back to Daisy. This was ridiculous. Since when had she started noticing a man's hands?

He gave an impatient sigh. 'Listen, Jenny, I don't—'

'Please, don't say anything else.' She stood up so quickly she almost knocked the chair flying, but she just couldn't bear to hear him list the reasons why he didn't want to be with her. 'I'd rather not talk about it.'

She'd rather not think about it either, but unfortunately that wasn't so easy.

She unstrapped Daisy and lifted her out of the high chair, cuddling her close. The feel of her soft, sturdy little body gave her courage.

'It was all my fault and I'm sorry.' She plucked up courage to look at him, trying to look relaxed about the whole thing. 'I was the one who gave you that stupid massage and I didn't think—I mean, it didn't occur to me that you'd—' She broke off and bit her lip, cursing her shyness. Everyone else seemed to be able to talk about sex. Why couldn't she? 'What I mean is, the kiss was all my fault and, please, don't think you've offended me by stopping when you did. You were Chloe's lover and I never should have—'

'I was never Chloe's lover,' he said impatiently, a frown touching his dark brows. 'And Chloe has absolutely nothing to do with what happened between you and I last night.'

'I still believe Daisy is your child,' she said hoarsely. 'The only thing that's changed is that you're not the man I first thought you were and I'm sorry I misjudged you.'

His longer fingers tapped a rhythm on the table. 'You didn't misjudge me.' His handsome face was inscrutable. 'I drink too much, I party too hard and I'm very careless about women's feelings. I've never had a relationship that's lasted longer than three months. I'm everything you believe me to be. You didn't misjudge me.'

She gave him what she hoped was a light-hearted smile. 'Well, at least I've taught you to eat breakfast.'

There was no answering smile in return. 'You've taught me more than that,' he drawled softly, his eyes never leaving her face. 'Like the fact that I do have a conscience. And that conscience, my dear Jenny, is the reason that you're still a virgin this morning.'

She was mortified that he'd guessed but after her reaction to him the night before it was hardly surprising.

'We wouldn't have—'

'Oh, yes, we would.' He drained his coffee. 'And I'm warning you to keep your distance, Red Riding Hood. The wolf let you escape last night. I can't guarantee it will happen a second time.'

Her heart banged hard against her ribs and her mouth was suddenly dry.

So he did find her attractive.

It wasn't just her that felt the special connection between them.

'I agree that you should move out,' Alex replied bluntly. 'There's no way I'll be able to keep my hands off you if you're continually wandering around my house.'

She stared at him. 'But I don't try to—'

'You really don't know much about men, do you?' he observed dryly. 'It's the fact that you're not trying that makes you so appealing. That and the fact that you have absolutely no idea how attractive you are. Even clothed, I'm struggling to keep my hands off you.'

Her stomach tumbled and she suddenly found breathing difficult. 'But I'm not doing anything.'

'You don't have to do anything,' Alex drawled. 'You can bath Daisy in an old T-shirt and I still want you. You can wear that ridiculous outfit that buttons from neck to hem and all I want to do is rip it off. The truth is that I have absolutely no interest in what you're wearing because all I want to do is rip it off, spread you on my bed and introduce you to the pleasures of sex. And now I've told you the truth, you'd better run.'

She stared at him, her breathing rapid, two spots of colour on her cheekbones.

He wanted to introduce her to the pleasures of sex?

No one had ever spoken to her in such a—such an explicit way before, and it did strange things to her insides.

'Alex—'

'Am I shocking you, Red Riding Hood?' His voice was silky smooth. 'Because I should be.'

Finally she found her voice. 'You're not shocking me. But you won't convince me that you're so wicked either. I know you now, Alex. I know you have a caring side.'

'Not in my relationships,' he said bluntly, and suddenly she realised her problem.

She'd come after him for Daisy, but now she'd got to know him she wanted him for *her*.

She was in love with Alex Westerling.

Appalled by the sudden revelation, she froze.

'You're right, of course,' she said finally, her lips stiff as she formed the words. 'You're not the right sort of man for me.'

And in a way she was telling the truth. For Alex a relationship was something purely physical. He didn't do the emotional stuff. How many times had he told her that?

There was a brief pause and his eyes burned into hers. 'Jenny—'

The soft chime of the doorbell interrupted whatever it was he'd intended to say and his darkened jaw tensed.

'Who the hell is that at this time of the morning?'

'Do you want me to go?' She looked at him anxiously. 'If it's a journalist I could tell them that you are out.'

He laughed out loud and flipped her cheek with a gentle finger. 'You are so damned innocent. What do you think a journalist would make of a pretty girl opening my door, holding a baby?'

Her eyes widened and she stared at him. 'I hadn't thought of that.'

'But fortunately I had.' He rose to his feet and walked towards the kitchen door. 'Better stay in here. Just in case.'

With that he closed the door firmly behind him, leaving her alone.

Jenny stared at Daisy helplessly. 'Oh, Daisy. What have I done? What on earth possessed me to fall in love with a man like him? I thought I had more sense than that.'

But the truth was that her emotions were outside her control for the first time in her life.

She hadn't chosen to fall in love with Alex Westerling but it had happened.

And who could blame her?

Alex was the ultimate catch. He had a mind like a rapier, he was sinfully good-looking and he could kiss a woman until she forgot her own name. He was good company and a surprisingly good listener. He was kind to his patients and a dedicated doctor. And he'd be a great father once he woke up to the fact that Daisy was his.

Not realising that she hadn't once thought about his money, Jenny tidied the kitchen with her free arm and then froze as she heard female laughter.

She felt as though she'd been showered with cold water.

Here she was, happily playing house and make believe, and she hadn't given any thought to Alex's current girl-friend. And there was bound to be one, of course. He just wasn't the sort of man to deny himself.

She dropped the cloth and held Daisy tighter, bracing herself as the door opened and Alex strolled in, his arm looped casually around the shoulders of a stunning blonde woman who was wearing the shortest skirt Jenny had ever seen.

Jenny tried to smile and she hoped that it looked more convincing than it felt.

'Hi, there—I'm Jenny.'

'And I'm Libby.' The girl looked at her curiously, switched her gaze to Daisy and then glanced at Alex.

'There's obviously quite a lot that you haven't been tell-ing me, you naughty boy.' Her voice was a seductive purr and her amazing blue eyes teased wickedly. 'I should drop in on you unannounced more often.'

'Not if you want to survive to old age,' Alex drawled, suppressing a yawn. 'Jenny, this is my sister Libby. Don't answer any of her questions. She's worse than any journalist.'

Sister?

Jenny wasn't sure which was worse. The pain of thinking that he was involved with this beautiful creature, or the intense feeling of joy that swamped her when she realised that he wasn't. If she'd needed conformation about the strength of her feelings for him, she had it now.

Alex poured a coffee and handed it to his sister. 'So, to what do I owe the honour? Have they run out of shoes in London?'

Libby laughed and sipped the coffee. 'No. I just happened to be passing.'

Alex lifted an eyebrow. 'Passing where? This is a dead end, Lib.'

Libby shrugged. 'All right. Actually, Andreas is away in Greece with Adrienne for a few days and I thought I'd take the opportunity to visit you.' She turned to smile at Jenny. 'Adrienne is Andreas's niece. She's seventeen.'

Alex looked at his sister suspiciously. 'And that's it?'

Her eyes twinkled naughtily. 'Well, Katy and I haven't heard a squeak from you lately and that's always a sign that you're otherwise occupied.'

Alex raised his eyes to heaven. 'And knowing that, you didn't think that I might want to be left in peace?'

'Absolutely not.' Libby smiled at Daisy. 'We're only staying for one night. I promise we won't be in the way. We'll just lounge on the beach.'

Jenny glanced between them, puzzled. 'We?'

'Libby has evidently brought my two nieces to visit me,' Alex said wearily, raking a hand through his dark hair and gazing at his sister in frustration. 'You really must learn to ring first.'

'Why?' His sister's gaze was disturbingly intent and Jenny suspected that there was something going on. 'Am I interrupting something?'

Alex hesitated for only the briefest second. 'No,' he said finally. 'But the nursery is already in use.'

Libby stared at him, momentarily struck dumb. 'But no one ever stays here.'

'Well, Jenny is staying here, with Daisy,' Alex said irritably, 'and you'd better get the girls out of the car, Lib.'

'They're asleep,' Libby said absent-mindedly, her eyes still on her brother. 'So are you saying there isn't room?'

Jenny cleared her throat. 'Of course there's room,' she said quickly. 'We can all share the nursery. This is Daisy. I'm sure she'll enjoy the company.'

'Pleased to meet you, Daisy.' Libby tickled the baby's cheek and made noises that drew a chuckle from the baby.

'I'll get the girls.'

Alex strode out of the room, leaving the two women together.

'I really, *really* didn't mean to intrude,' Libby said softly, her tone contrite. 'I had no idea. Alex never invites women back here. If he invited you then you must be very special.'

Jenny closed her eyes briefly. What was she supposed to say?

She could hardly confess that Alex hadn't invited her. That she'd landed herself on him together with a paternity suit and that life had never seemed more complicated than it was at the moment.

Fortunately Alex was back in the kitchen within minutes, carrying two little girls in his arms.

They cuddled against him sleepily and he dropped a kiss on each of their dark curls before handing them to Libby.

'We really need to go to work. You know where everything is.' He gave a wry smile. 'I don't need to tell you to

make yourself at home because you always do. We'll see
you later.'

'We?' Libby was clearly consumed by curiosity and
Alex let out a breath.

'Jenny works in the same department as me. Now let it
go, Lib.'

'So you met at work?'

Jenny threw a helpless glance at Alex who rolled his
eyes.

'How we met is none of your damned business.'

Libby gasped and covered the older child's ears.
'Alexander Westerling, you shouldn't use language like
that in front of my four-year-old!!'

'Then you shouldn't bring her to stay with her wicked
uncle unannounced,' Alex drawled, but he stooped to kiss
the girls. 'See you later. We'll go and play in the sand.'

The youngest one gazed up at him. 'Thand castles?'

'Definitely thand castles,' Alex mimicked gently, reaching out to pick up his car keys from the table. 'Have a good
day and don't get up to any mischief.'

The moment she'd dropped Daisy at the crèche Jenny went
in search of Alex.

She found him in the treatment room, examining a
wound that had come in to be redressed.

'It's infected,' he was saying in that definite voice he
always used. 'I'll give you antibiotics and you need to come
back and get it checked.' He broke off briefly when he saw
Jenny hovering anxiously in the doorway and then turned
his attention back to the patient, finishing his instructions.

Then he strolled over to Jenny, his handsome face blank
of expression. 'My office. Now.'

She blinked and wondered whether she'd ever get used
to the way Alex always had to be in control.

But she had little choice other than to follow him through

to his office, and she had to admit that they needed privacy for the conversation that they were about to have.

She closed the door quietly behind her and hovered in front of it.

'You'd better sit down.' Alex collapsed into the chair behind his desk and closed his eyes. He looked worn out and it struck her that he was still obviously recovering from his bout of flu. 'I suppose you want to talk about my damned sister.'

Jenny bit her lip. 'I just don't know what we're going to say to her.'

Alex yawned. 'Why do we need to say anything to her?'

How could he be so relaxed?

'She'll want an explanation.'

'I never explain myself to anyone,' he said in a cool tone, and then sighed. 'Don't look so worried, Red Riding Hood. You're still safe in the wolf's lair, remember? I'll sort it out.'

'But what will you tell her?'

Alex shrugged, totally indifferent to what she saw as a massive problem. 'I don't know. I'm not in the habit of discussing my relationships with my sister.'

Jenny coloured. 'But we're not having a relationship.'

He shot her a strange look. 'No, we're not, are we? Yet.'

His smooth tones heated her blood and she felt warmth spread through her body.

'I—I'll try and find a flat today,' she croaked, and he gave a short laugh.

'You'll be lucky. This is a tourist resort in the middle of the tourist season. You'll be lucky even to find a metre of sand that someone hasn't already bagged.'

'But you said—'

'Yeah, I know what I said.' He gave a wry smile. 'It's certainly safer if you move out but seeing that isn't going to be possible we'll have to go with the more dangerous option.'

'What do you mean?'

'You continuing to live with the wolf,' he said slowly, leaning forward and looking at her with an intensity that made her pulse accelerate alarmingly. 'Until we find out about Daisy.'

Jenny stared at him, heart pounding. 'She's yours, Alex.'

'So you keep saying.' A muscle worked in his lean jaw. 'I think for both our sakes it's time we found out the truth so that we can get on with our lives.'

CHAPTER EIGHT

JENNY arrived home from work first and found Libby feeding both children in the kitchen.

Alex's usually pristine bachelor environment had been transformed into a girly paradise. Shoes seemed to be scattered everywhere, items of clothing had been dropped haphazardly on the floor and the kitchen looked as though someone had used a blender without the lid.

'I'm afraid that's Athena's fault,' Libby explained cheerfully, following the direction of Jenny's gaze. 'She's a terribly messy eater. Don't worry. Alex is used to her. There's no point in clearing it up halfway through. I always wait until she's finished. Then we get the hose out.'

Jenny giggled. 'I bet Alex has a shock when you come to stay.'

'He just reaches for the whisky bottle,' Libby said dryly, smiling tolerantly as Athena grabbed a handful of pasta and rubbed it into the table. 'My husband, Andreas, is the same. He adores the girls but he's a typical macho Greek. He doesn't know one end of a nappy from the other. Which is utterly ridiculous because the guy is a paediatrician and an incredibly good one at that. He just isn't great at the practical stuff. A bit like Alex.'

Not like Alex.

Jenny slipped Daisy into the high chair, thinking that Libby would be surprised if she knew just how involved Alex had been with Daisy.

After that first night, when she'd forced the issue, he often helped out with her and seemed to relish spending time with the baby.

140

'She's beautiful,' Libby said, her eyes resting on Daisy thoughtfully. 'How old?'

'Six months. How old is Athena?'

'Just two.' Libby pulled a face. 'And Zoe is four. Jolly hard work, I can tell you. I used to work on a paediatric ward. I can't imagine how I used to look after twenty-four little patients. I can't manage two when they're mine. Fortunately my husband is addicted to his daughters so I get some help once he's home. That's why I run to Alex when Andreas is away. I can't cope on my own. Pathetic.'

'They're gorgeous,' Jenny said wistfully, thinking how lucky the children were to have two parents who adored each other. Daisy would never have that.

'They're both horribly spoilt,' Libby admitted, smiling indulgently, 'Andreas is Greek and he adores his little girls. Of which I'm one, fortunately.'

Jenny smiled. She could well imagine it. Libby was the girliest 'girl' she'd ever met and so bubbly that you wanted to put the lid on her in case she fizzed over the carpet.

'So come on—' Libby's eyes gleamed mischievously '—tell me everything about Alex.'

Jenny tensed. 'There's nothing to tell.'

'Oh, come on…' Libby slipped her shoes off and curled her legs under her on the chair, obviously totally at home. 'Jenny, my brother has never invited a woman into his home before. I want to know why you're the exception.'

Jenny chewed her lip. 'I'm not exactly the exception. You see, it's—it's—'

'None of her business,' came a deep, dark drawl from the doorway. 'Back off, Elizabeth.'

His tone contained a definite warning and Libby pouted.

'You're a horrible grouch and I can't think why I ever come and visit you.'

'You come and visit me because your husband is away and you don't want Athena to make that sort of mess in your own kitchen.' Alex strolled into the kitchen and stopped in front of his niece, frowning deeply. 'I wish you'd stop using my walls for target practice, madam.'

Athena chuckled happily and reached up to him with gooey hands. 'Lexth, lexth—cuggle—'

Alex leaned down and dropped a kiss on her curly head, keeping a safe distance from her chubby hands. 'I never cuddle my women while they're covered in tomato sauce,' he said dryly. 'When your mother has hosed you down we'll have a cuddle.'

He sat down next to Zoe.

'Hi, there, Zoe. How are you doing?'

'Good, Uncle Alex.' The little girl smiled up at him. 'Can we go to the beach?'

'Sure.' Alex glanced at Libby and lifted an eyebrow. 'Is that OK with you?'

She beamed. 'Definitely. We'll all go. Or is that a problem for Daisy?'

'Daisy loves the beach,' Jenny said quickly. 'She eats the sand.'

'They all do at that age,' Libby said sagely, and Alex rolled his eyes.

'Athena still eats it. In fact, that girl eats everything.'

Jenny stood up. 'I'll make up a bottle for Daisy and heat up her food here.' She bustled around the kitchen, preparing what she needed, clearing up as she went.

Libby stood up and lifted Athena off the chair. 'Oh, yuck. I wonder if you actually ate anything. Most of it seems to be stuck to your bottom.'

'Her aim is hopeless,' Alex said mildly, observing the food stuck to the floor and the walls. 'She has absolutely no idea where her mouth is.'

Libby laughed and reached for a cloth to wipe Athena's face and hands. 'She does when it's chocolate. She never misses.'

'Now, why doesn't that surprise me?' Alex rolled his

eyes and reached into the fridge for some beer. Then he glanced at Jenny, his gaze gently mocking.

Jenny blushed and gave a shy smile. She knew that he was challenging her to scold him for drinking but she had no intention of doing any such thing. Instead, she reached out a hand to take the bottles of lager.

'You can put those in Daisy's bag,' she said calmly, and he gave a reluctant smile.

'Put one in for me,' Libby said, turning Athena round to check she hadn't missed any splodges of tomato. 'There we are, you're clean.'

'Clean?' Alex surveyed his niece and raised an eyebrow. 'You seriously call that clean?'

'It's clean for Athena, Uncle Alex,' Zoe said solemnly, and he laughed and swung her into his arms.

'I suppose it is, sweetheart. Now, then, what are we going to do on the beach?'

'Can we go over by the cliffs and play caves?'

Alex nodded. 'Sounds good to me.'

He held onto her and Jenny watched them, a lump building in her throat.

How could he possibly think he wouldn't make a good father? He was so lovely with his nieces. He would have made an absolutely wonderful father for Daisy. Except that he was determined to deny that she was his. She remembered his comments about contacting his lawyer and wondered whether he'd had any news during the day.

Presumably not or he would have mentioned it.

On the other hand, he would hardly have mentioned it at work and he wasn't in a position to bring it up now because Libby was staying there.

She shifted Daisy slightly, wondering how he'd react when his lawyer confirmed that there was every possibility that he was the baby's father.

She'd have to move out, of course.

There was no way they could continue to live together.

They'd have to come to some arrangement whereby he could continue to see Daisy regularly.

And as for her—well, she'd only see him on an occasional basis.

She felt as though a heavy lump of lead was sitting in her stomach. The thought of leaving Alex dismayed her more than she could ever have imagined.

She'd dismissed him as a superficial playboy but the truth was that there was nothing superficial about Alex. Nothing at all.

He was incredibly complex.

On the surface he was sophisticated and independent, the ultimate Mr Cool, a man who possessed a wild streak that had earned him a wicked reputation. But underneath there was so much more to him. He had a brilliant brain, a sharp sense of humour and was capable of great warmth towards those in trouble. He was impatient with freeloaders and the press but who could blame him for that?

She'd even started to understand his womanising. He was a stunningly good-looking man who'd been born to one of the richest families in Britain. It was hardly any wonder he'd had a string of girlfriends.

But he hadn't made a commitment to any of them, she reminded herself gloomily.

That was one aspect of his personality that she couldn't understand.

Despite his caustic comments about children, he was actually very good with them.

So why had he never settled down?

Despite the fact that it was late afternoon, the beach was still crowded and they found themselves a spot near to the caves that Zoe was keen to explore.

Libby settled herself on the sand with Athena and let the toddler play with a bucket and spade while Jenny snuggled Daisy on her lap and gave her a bottle.

Alex took Zoe's hand and they wandered off inside the cave.

'You know, Katy and I always said that Alex would end up with someone small and dark. No, don't eat the sand, darling.' Libby leaned forward to brush the sand away from Athena's mouth. 'Yuck. Amazing, isn't it? Her dinner doesn't make it anywhere near her mouth but with the sand she's spot on. Dig, Athena. Dig. Not eat. He's always dated blondes.'

Jenny tried not to mind about that. 'Libby, we're not exactly dating, we're—'

'Well, there's something going on,' Libby said calmly. 'I've known Alex for thirty-four years and I've never known him protect a woman the way he protects you. The slightest whiff of an uncomfortable situation and he dives in and rescues you.'

Jenny frowned. Did he? She'd never even thought about it.

'Truly, we're not—'

'Jenny—' Libby's tone was patient '—I can see you're in love with him. Every time you look at him it shines out of your eyes.'

Jenny stared at her, appalled. Her first instinct was to deny it and then she realised helplessly that there was probably no point and anyway her main concern wasn't Libby.

'Do you think your brother knows?' she croaked, glancing towards the cave to check that Alex wasn't within earshot.

Libby looked taken aback. 'I don't know. Probably. Women are always in love with him, so he sort of expects it. But what's the problem? He's clearly crazy about you too.'

Crazy about *her*?'

Jenny shook her head. 'No. He isn't. It isn't like that.'

It was true that he seemed to be attracted to her for some

reason, but she didn't fool herself that it was anything other than novelty value.

Libby brushed some more sand away from Athena's face but her eyes were on Jenny. 'Why don't you tell me what's going on?'

It was severely tempting to confide in someone who knew Alex well but Jenny shook her head.

The issue of Daisy was between her and Alex and she didn't feel comfortable sharing it with anyone else until Alex chose to acknowledge his responsibility for Daisy. And as for the other issue—her relationship with Alex—there was absolutely nothing going on.

Unfortunately.

Libby was looking at her with sympathy. 'Well, if it's any consolation, he seems to treat you differently to all the other women he's ever been with.'

Jenny concentrated on Daisy, not wanting to think about the other women that Alex had been with. It just hurt too much.

Daisy finished the bottle and Jenny and Libby chatted casually until Alex arrived back with an excited Zoe.

'We went right into the cave and it was so *dark*,' she said, her voice an awed whisper. 'Uncle Alex was scared so I had to hold his hand.'

Libby laughed and then gave a startled gasp and lifted her hand to her neck, knocking off an enormous bee that had landed on her skin.

Her face blanched and she jumped to her feet, her expression one of pure panic as she looked at her brother. 'Alex, I've been stung.'

Alex was by her side immediately, his expression grim. 'Jenny, call the air ambulance *now*! Tell them we've got a case of anaphylactic shock.' He took his sister by the shoulders and looked down at her, his tone urgent. 'Where? Where did it sting you?'

For a moment Jenny stood frozen to the spot, uncomprehending, and then she fumbled in her bag for her mobile phone and dialled the emergency number without question. She had no idea what was going on but she knew better than to doubt Alex about anything medical. If he felt that he needed the air ambulance then he needed it.

As she slipped the phone back in her bag, Zoe caught her hand, her eyes terrified.

'Mummy's allergic to bees,' she said, her little voice trembling.

Allergic to bees?

Jenny glanced at Alex in horror but all his attention was on his sister.

'Where did it sting you, Lib?'

'Neck.' Libby was white and Alex tipped her head over and examined the skin.

'I see it. The sting is still in there.'

'Get it out! Alex, get it out!' Libby was gasping now and Alex scraped at the sting with his finger until he finally managed to remove it.

'It's out. Tell me you're carrying adrenaline,' he said through gritted teeth, and Libby nodded, lifting a hand to her throat, her eyes wide with panic.

'It's starting. I can feel it. I can't breathe, Alex. Oh, no, *I can't breathe.*'

She started to gasp and sob, clutching at him with her free hand, and he scooped her up in his arms and laid her gently on the blanket.

'It's all right, baby, I'm here.' His voice was rock solid and reassuring but Jenny noticed his hand shaking slightly as he reached out to grasp Libby's bag. Jaw clenched tight, he lifted it and emptied the contents unceremoniously onto the rug. 'You're going to be fine, sweetheart. Try not to panic.'

'My throat…' Libby's voice was a rasp as she clutched at her brother's shoulders.

'It's OK, Lib— I'm here, sweetheart. Jenny, find the adrenaline,' he growled. *'Quickly!'*

The gravity of the scenario swamping her with horror, Jenny dropped to her knees and rummaged through the contents of Libby's handbag, her hands shaking so badly that she couldn't grasp anything. There seemed to be thousands of different lipsticks, notebooks, numerous screwed-up chocolate wrappers, but finally her fingers closed around a pre-loaded syringe of adrenaline.

By now Libby was gasping and her face was swelling rapidly. She clutched her brother, her eyes terrified as she stared up at him desperately. 'Don't let me die! Don't let me die, Alex.'

'You're not going to die, baby,' Alex soothed, snapping his fingers at Jenny in an attempt to hurry her.

Sick with reaction, Jenny pushed the syringe into his hand and he sucked in a breath as he jabbed the syringe into Libby's thigh without a second's hesitation. 'You're not going to die, Libby. I promise you won't die.'

Jenny watched in appalled silence, frozen to the spot in shock. Only moments earlier they'd been chatting happily and now Libby was fighting for every breath.

In all her years working in A and E Libby had never seen anyone deteriorate so quickly. It was a nightmare of the worst proportions and she didn't need to see Alex's white face to know just how gravely ill his sister was.

'Uncle Alex…?' Zoe's voice quivered. 'What's happening to Mummy?'

Jenny gave a gasp of horror and scooped the child into her arms. In the urgency of the situation, they'd both forgotten the children.

'Mummy will be fine, angel,' Alex said firmly, giving the little girl a quick smile before transferring his gaze to Jenny.

'Get the children away.' His voice was remarkably calm. 'Ask that family over there to look after them for a minute and then get yourself back over here. I'm going to need your help.'

Jenny did as he ordered, her palms clammy as she ushered the children to the family sitting near them on the beach.

Zoe was trying to ask more questions but fortunately the other family immediately saw the problem and took over, comforting and distracting the little girl.

By the time she'd sprinted back to Alex, Libby was barely conscious. Her lips were tinged blue and she was wheezing badly.

Alex was trying to reassure her but Jenny could see the tension in his broad shoulders.

'The adrenaline hasn't touched her and I don't have any with me. I left it in the house. Everything is swelling up,' he muttered, raking long fingers through her hair in a gesture of frustration. 'Go through her handbag again and see if you can find hydrocortisone. I told her to carry both.'

Frantically hoping that Libby had followed her brother's advice, Jenny pushed aside lipsticks, mirrors, nail varnish, ribbons and closed her fingers around an ampoule of hydrocortisone and a syringe.

'I've got it!'

'Draw it up,' Alex ordered, struggling to keep Libby's airway patent.

Jenny did as he asked and handed him the syringe.

'I can't stop what I'm doing—you're going to have to do it,' he said immediately. 'She carries a tourniquet. Put it on her arm and find a vein. I want you to give it IV. *Where the hell is that helicopter?*'

Jenny didn't argue but she was suddenly terrified that she wouldn't be able to do what he asked.

Working in a well-equipped accident and emergency department was very different to delivering lifesaving first aid on a beach. Especially when the victim was someone you knew.

Her hands were shaking and she felt physically sick.

She tightened the tourniquet, aware of the sound of a helicopter in the distance.

By now a small crowd had gathered and Alex was giving instructions.

'Make an "X" in the sand so that they can land, and clear everyone away! Hurry!'

Jenny concentrated on Libby's arm. 'That looks like a good vein.'

Please, let it be a good vein.

'Go for it. And don't miss.' Alex lifted his eyes and his gaze burned into hers, giving her courage. 'Good girl. You can do it.'

She swallowed hard and then swabbed the skin and picked up the syringe. She pushed the needle, felt the skin give and then she was in the vein.

'Well done.' Alex was still watching. 'Now inject it— that's right. A bit faster.'

As Libby removed the syringe, the paramedics sprinted up to them with oxygen.

Alex grabbed it and covered Libby's mouth and nose with the mask. 'Get me some more adrenaline,' he ordered swiftly. 'I've given her one lot and it's done nothing. I want to try some more.' He turned his attention back to his sister, stroking her hair and talking gently to her while maintaining her compromised airway. 'If this doesn't work I'll need to intubate her.'

He swore softly, the strain clearly visible on his handsome face, and Jenny stood watching, totally powerless to help as the paramedics handed Alex a syringe.

He gave Libby another injection of adrenaline. 'Come on, sweetheart,' he said calmly, discarding the empty syringe and smoothing Libby's blonde hair away from her forehead with a hand that wasn't quite steady.

As if in response to his voice, Libby's eyes flickered open and she started to retch.

Alex let out a breath and immediately turned her on her side. 'Good girl. You're going to be fine. I'm here, sweetheart. I'm here.'

Hearing the shake in his usually confident voice, Jenny felt her eyes fill. If she'd ever doubted that Alex was capable of love, those doubts had now gone. His love for his sister was obvious to all watching.

He looked at the paramedics, his face white. 'I'm coming with you and we need to be prepared to intubate her. Can you call ahead and warn the unit that we're bringing in a severe case of anaphylactic shock caused by a bee sting?'

Alex turned his attention back to Libby who seemed to be improving by the minute.

The swelling around her mouth and tongue had reduced slightly and at last she appeared to be aware of what was going on.

'Alex—'

'You're going to be OK, sweetheart,' he said hoarsely, running a hand over his rough jaw. 'You're going to be fine. Which is more than can be said for the rest of us. You gave us the fright of our lives. Do that to me again and I'll bloody well kill you myself.'

But he held onto his sister's hand tightly and there was no missing the depth of love in his eyes as he watched her closely, checking that her condition continued to improve.

He looked totally wrung out and it was hardly surprising. Handling a medical emergency on a public beach was stressful enough, without the patient being an adored sister.

Libby didn't respond for a moment and then she tried to speak again. 'The girls—'

'I'll take them,' Jenny said quickly, placing a hand on Alex's shoulder in a gesture of sympathy. 'I'll stay with them for as long as you need me to.'

At the very least she could do that. She wished she could do more. Anything to ease the tension in Alex's shoulders.

The paramedics were back with a stretcher and Jenny stood to one side while they prepared to lift Libby.

'I'm going to need to stay with her,' Alex said, his eyes still on his sister, and Jenny nodded.

'Of course. Stay as long as you need to.'

'I'll call Andreas from the hospital.' He turned to her with a harassed smile. 'I'm landing you with three children, Red Riding Hood.'

She gave a calm smile. 'I can cope with three children.'

'Athena is a monkey.'

'I can cope. You just worry about Libby.'

'I am.' He let out a breath and then shook his head slowly. 'Thanks, Jenny.'

'No thanks needed,' she whispered, but he was back beside Libby, checking her airway, talking to her, reassuring her while they carried her across the sand to the waiting helicopter.

Once it took off the crowd dispersed and Jenny thanked the family that had taken the three children.

'Will Mummy die?' Zoe looked at her with huge eyes, her lower lip trembling ominously.

'No, darling.' Jenny stooped to hug her, feeling her own tears start. It had been a horrifying, frightening experience for all of them, especially the children. 'Uncle Alex has already made her better. They're just taking her to hospital to give her some more medicine.'

And to be ready if she relapsed. Oh, God…

Zoe nodded solemnly. 'Uncle Alex is very clever. Mummy and Daddy told me that. He'd never let Mummy die.'

Jenny brushed the tears away from her cheeks. She didn't even want to think about Libby dying, but she knew just how close it had been.

Aware of her responsibility to Libby's children, she

made a huge effort and managed what she hoped was a relatively normal smile. 'He is clever. Very clever. Now, then, how do you fancy going home and playing an amazing game in the bath?'

CHAPTER NINE

IT WAS two next morning when Alex finally arrived home.

The children were fast asleep together in the nursery and Jenny was lying on her bed, reading.

The moment she heard his footsteps on the stairs she put the book down and held her breath. She'd been longing for news but she hadn't wanted to call the hospital and disturb Alex so she'd forced herself to be patient.

He paused in the entrance to her bedroom, his broad shoulders filling the doorway.

'I thought you'd be asleep.'

'I was too worried about Libby,' she confessed shakily, 'and I wanted to listen out for the children. Particularly Zoe. She's old enough to understand that her mummy is really ill. We talked about it and I think she was all right, but I've been worried she might wake up and go looking for Libby.'

His eyes glittered strangely in the semi-darkness. 'You're a good, kind person, Red Riding Hood.'

Jenny shook her head. 'I felt totally useless out there on the beach.'

'You weren't useless,' he said gruffly. 'You did a good job.'

Jenny's eyes filled. 'It was so awful.'

He held out his arms and she went into them, feeling the reassuring warmth and hardness of his chest against her cheek.

'How is she?'

'Off the critical list, I hope.'

She lifted her head and even in the limited light she could see the evidence of stress in his handsome features. Given that he'd been ill with flu only days earlier, it was amazing that he was still standing. 'We're keeping her in hospital for twenty-four hours at least because people can have prolonged reactions and I'm not taking any chances. Andreas is flying back now. He should be here in the morning.'

Libby bit her lip. 'You saved her life.'

Alex gave a laugh that was totally lacking in humour. 'Unfortunately it isn't the first time. It happened once before, at one of my parents' wretched garden parties. None of us knew she was even allergic to bee stings before then. She collapsed and, of course, we had nothing. No adrenaline. Nothing. It was touch and go.'

'So now she always carries adrenaline?'

Alex nodded. 'Thank goodness. Although I'm going to tell her that she needs to carry more than one syringe of the stuff.'

Jenny lifted hand and touched his cheek gently. 'You must feel worn out after that. I can't imagine what it must have felt like, seeing your sister collapse like that.'

'It was traumatic,' he muttered wearily, and she shrugged helplessly.

'Can I get you anything? A whisky?'

Despite the obvious tension, he gave a soft laugh. 'You're actually offering to pour me a whisky?'

She gave a hesitant smile. 'I think you need to relax. If it didn't taste so revolting I'd have one myself.'

His blue eyes burned into hers. 'And what if I prefer to use one of your other methods?'

Her breath caught at the look in his eyes and she felt her legs wobble. 'Which method did you have in mind?'

He hesitated for a long moment and then he gave a groan and slid his hands into her hair, pulling her hard against him.

She held her breath, aching with anticipation as she waited for his kiss, but he just stared down at her, his expression inscrutable.

'You are such a gentle, kind person, Jenny,' he muttered hoarsely, 'and I am totally wrong for you.'

The blood was pounding in her ears and her insides melted. 'You're not wrong for me.'

He stroked her hair away from her face, his eyes devouring hers. 'I can't give you a relationship.'

'I know that.'

His breathing was unsteady. 'So why aren't you running?'

'Because I love you,' she said simply, and he closed his eyes and gave a groan.

'Jenny…'

'It's OK,' she whispered. 'I'm not asking anything of you. I just wanted to be honest with you. I know you don't love me back. I don't expect you to.'

Suddenly she didn't care about his relationship with her sister. Being with Alex felt totally right.

For this one night, they were meant to be together.

He opened his eyes and his hands tightened on her face. 'You don't know what you're saying.'

'Oh, yes, I do.' She gave a shy smile. 'I know exactly what I'm saying.'

Breathing heavily, he lowered his forehead to hers. She could feel the hard bite of his fingers through the thin fabric of her T-shirt and the warmth of his powerful body pressing against hers. The excitement was so intense that it threatened to swamp her.

'The children…'

'Athena and Zoe never wake up,' he muttered, inhaling her scent as he kissed his way down her neck.

'Alex…' She gasped his name and lifted her hands, terrified that her legs wouldn't hold her any longer. But fortunately they didn't have to. He scooped her up easily into his arms and carried her into his bedroom, laying her gently on his bed before coming down on top of her.

He was all powerful muscle and hard male strength and

she felt her heart pound uncontrollably as she placed her hands on his arms in a gesture of pure female surrender.

She stared up at him, her fingers digging into the curves of his biceps, waiting, wanting, and finally he lowered his head and kissed her.

His mouth played gently with hers and his tongue flickered out and traced the seam of her lips until she opened to him with a gasp of longing. He delved deeper, exploring her mouth with a thoroughness that left her trembling and clutching his shoulders. He pulled away for just long enough to strip off his clothes and then she felt the smooth slide of his hand on her T-shirt. He removed it in a swift movement and then he was touching her breast, teasing her nipple until moist heat pooled between her thighs.

Alex dragged his mouth away from hers and she briefly caught the glitter of his eyes before he shifted himself slightly so that he could gaze at her breasts.

'I'm really flat-chested,' she joked feebly, and he lifted his head and his eyes burned into hers.

'You're absolutely beautiful,' he said hoarsely. 'Don't ever believe anything different. And you have gorgeous breasts.'

She lay still, transfixed by the expression in his eyes, knowing that he meant it. And the knowledge made her feel more like a woman than she ever had before.

And then he lowered his head to her breast and heat exploded in her belly. With a skilled flick of his clever tongue he teased one pink nipple while his fingers played gently with the other. Her response was instantaneous, her hips shifting restlessly against the cool sheets in an effort to relieve the building pressure in her pelvis. The excitement was so intense that she thought she'd explode and perhaps he knew that because he ceased the flicking motion and instead drew her nipple into the damp heat of his mouth.

Jenny's whole body burned with longing.

She writhed and sobbed underneath him, clutching at his dark hair in a fevered desperation.

'Alex…'

He lifted his head, his blue eyes suddenly fierce. 'Don't ever tell me you're not attractive,' he said thickly, his thumb slowly tracing the contour of her damp, pouting nipple. 'You're incredible. And intensely sexual.'

Her breath was coming in pants. 'Alex, please…'

'Please, what?'

'I need you to—' She broke off, unable to believe that she was being so brazen. 'Please, touch me—please…'

Alex shifted slightly so that he was looking directly down at her and then his hand slid down her heated flesh, impatiently removed the barrier of her panties and then returned to rest lightly on the dark curls that protected the heart of her femininity.

'Is this what you want?'

This time, instead of stopping him she arched against him, her whole body begging for his touch, encouraging him.

His eyes locked on hers, increasing the intimacy as he parted her legs with long, clever fingers, caressing her with a sure touch.

She gasped, her hands biting into the powerful muscles of his shoulders, unable to look away from the raw sexual need that glittered in those blue eyes.

His gaze stripped her naked, both physically and emotionally, and the knowledge that there were no barriers between them left her heady with excitement.

Amazingly she felt no shyness, only a sinful desire to know this man in every possible sense.

She stroked her fingers over the dark hair that covered his chest, tracing its course down his sleek, heated flesh until finally they brushed gently over the throbbing heat of his arousal.

He gave a harsh groan and she touched him as she'd

never touched a man before, intrigued by the silken heat that pulsed in her seeking hand. Gently she explored him, her eyes still locked with his, the blood pulsing in her veins as she learned his power and masculinity.

'Jenny, I can't...' He eased away from her, his breathing rapid. 'You have to give me a minute.'

'No!' She coiled her legs around him in explicit invitation but the muscles of his shoulders bunched and he held himself away from her.

'Not yet—you're not ready.'

Not ready?

How much more ready could she get?

She gave a sob of frustration, lifting her hips towards his in desperation, but he ignored her seductive movement and slid downwards, intent on tormenting her still further.

She'd thought that excitement had pushed her beyond shyness but when she felt the cool flick of his tongue against the damp core of her womanhood she tensed and tried to wriggle away from him, but he held her firm, ignoring her shocked protests. His hands holding her still, he took what he wanted, exploring her in the most intimate way possible until she forgot about shyness, consumed by an excitement more powerful and delicious than she could possibly have imagined.

And then finally, when she felt the pulses start deep inside her, he slid back up the bed and took her mouth, his kiss both erotic and explicit as he moved over her, his weight on his elbows.

'Curl your legs around me,' he ordered roughly, and she did as he instructed, in the grip of sensations totally beyond her control.

It was going to happen...

Finally, now, it was going to happen...

Alex hesitated briefly, staring down into her face, and suddenly she was terrified that he was going to change his mind again. Terrified that she wouldn't please him.

Her fingers slid down the sleek skin of his back, urging him forward, bringing him closer to her feminine heat, and with a sharply indrawn breath he slid an arm under her hips and lifted her, positioning her to take him.

She tensed as she felt the hard probe of his shaft against her and then he thrust gently, pausing to allow her to accommodate him before deepening his possession. She felt herself open to him, relishing each movement, feeling his pulsing strength as she drew him in.

He paused, his breathing unsteady, a sheen of sweat on his brow as he stared down at her, his eyes fierce with restrained passion.

'Am I hurting you?'

She shook her head and urged him closer, refusing to acknowledge the flash of pain that tried to intrude on the rising heat of her excitement.

But he must have felt her body's faint resistance to the alien male intrusion because he swore softly and smoothed her dampened hair away from her face with a hand that was far from steady.

'Relax, sweetheart,' he urged hoarsely, and she did as he instructed, hypnotised by the look in his blue eyes. 'Better?'

She nodded, everything she felt reflected in her eyes as she gazed up at him, and he closed his eyes and moved deeply within her.

'You're mine now, Jenny,' he groaned hoarsely, each movement of his hips taking him deeper, building the tension. 'All mine.'

Her eyes closed.

All his.

She wanted so much for it to be true and for this one, wild, suspended moment in time she surrendered to the fantasy and clung to him, feeling the tiny shivers build within her as he drove them both to a peak of pulsing ecstasy that seemed to last for ever.

Sated and limp, she clung to the sleek muscle of his

shoulders, relishing each moment of their intimacy, knowing that it couldn't last.

How could it?

He wouldn't want the children to find them like this, locked together, when they padded into his bedroom in the morning, and neither would she.

And despite the fiercely possessive words he'd spoken at the height of passion, she knew that, for him, the night had just been a lush oasis of pleasure in an otherwise barren day of stress and anxiety.

He rolled onto his back, taking her with him, holding her tight against his hair roughened chest.

'You are amazing.' He slipped his fingers under her chin and forced her to look at him, his expression stunned. 'Jenny…'

'Shh…' She placed a finger over his lips, wanting to stop him before he said something that would pierce the bubble of happiness that still bloomed inside her. 'Let's not talk about it.'

Alex gave a totally male smile. 'Trust you to be different,' he said gruffly, snuggling her back into the crook of his arm. 'A woman who doesn't want to talk after sex.'

Jenny felt a tiny stab of disappointment.

Sex.

Of course, that's all it would have been to Alex. What else had she expected? That after enjoying one night of passion with her he'd suddenly discover that all his years of avoiding women had been for the express purpose of keeping himself free for *her*?

She slid an arm around him, desperate to hold onto him for as long as possible. For tonight, at least, he was hers. And if that was all she could ever have of Alex then she was going to relish every minute.

Jenny awoke feeling warm and comfortable and realised that she was still snuggled against Alex, her limbs tangled with his. She moved her head and glanced at the clock. Five o'clock. Still early for grown-ups but not small children and she had three of them to look after.

Conscious that she didn't want them to find her in Alex's bed, she slid away from him, trying not to wake him, quickly retrieved her discarded T-shirt from the floor and hurried back to her own room.

She was only just in time.

Within minutes she heard Athena cry out and tiptoed into the nursery to see if she could settle her down again.

But the little girl was wide awake and ready to play, and her cries had woken Daisy who was suddenly equally alert.

Resigning herself to an early start, Jenny lifted Daisy out of her cot and took the two youngest children down to the living room to play.

She didn't want them to wake Alex.

Remembering just how little sleep he'd had the night before, her face heated and she gave a wistful sigh.

She'd thought that one night with Alex was better than none but now she wasn't so sure. He'd taught her more about her body in one night than she'd learned by herself in twenty-three years. He'd released a part of herself that she hadn't known existed and now it was loose she didn't know how to handle it.

She felt like a different person—her whole being focused on the feminine part of herself that he'd awakened with his clever touch.

For the first time in her life she felt like a real woman. An attractive, flesh-and-blood woman.

Restless and tense after everything that had happened, she took the children into the kitchen, strapped Daisy into the high chair and let Athena help her make bread.

She nipped upstairs once to check on Zoe and found her curled up in bed with Alex, both of them fast asleep.

Jenny looked at the two of them and felt her heart turn over.

If Alex truly thought he'd be a bad father then he was fooling himself.

He'd be a fantastic father.

She walked quietly back downstairs, leaving the two of them sleeping and they eventually emerged at eight o'clock, yawning and tousled. Zoe was still in her pyjamas and Alex had pulled on a pair of jeans.

Unshaven and with his chest bare, he looked breathtakingly attractive and Jenny blushed as she caught his eye.

She had absolutely no experience of morning-after conversation. Fortunately the presence of the children made everything easier.

'Athena and I have made rolls,' she said cheerfully, and Alex glanced round his kitchen with a wry smile.

'So I see. Did any of the dough make it into the oven?'

'Just a bit.' Jenny smiled. 'She woke very early and I wanted to keep her busy so that she didn't…well…'

Alex nodded to indicate that he'd understood that she hadn't wanted the little girl to miss her mother's presence.

He stooped to put Zoe in one of the kitchen chairs and then stretched, and Jenny's eyes were drawn to the ripple of muscle in his shoulders. He had a fantastic body and just remembering what he'd made her feel in bed made her shiver with longing.

Suddenly she was aware of every unfamiliar ache of her body.

He looked at her keenly. 'Are you OK?'

She knew exactly what he was asking and met his gaze boldly. 'Very OK.'

Not for a moment did she want him thinking that she regretted what had happened between them.

How could she possibly regret anything so utterly perfect?

There was an expression in his eyes that she couldn't interpret. 'Good.' His eyes searched hers for a moment longer and then he reached across the table for a roll and put one on a plate for Zoe. 'I've spoken to Andreas. He arrived during the night and went straight to the hospital.'

Jenny poured some milk for Zoe. 'He was lucky he was able to get a flight so quickly.'

'His family has a private jet,' Alex said in such a matter-of-fact voice that Jenny felt herself deflate like an overfilled balloon.

He'd mentioned the private jet with a total lack of interest. If ever she'd needed a reminder of the difference in their social circumstances then he'd just provided one.

What was she doing with this man?

He moved in circles that were so far removed from her own that it was ridiculous. Their paths never would have crossed if it hadn't been for Chloe.

But even knowing that, she couldn't regret what had happened the night before.

Oblivious to her distress, Alex drank a mug of coffee and then stood up. 'I'm going back to the hospital. Are you OK here with the children?'

Jenny nodded. 'Of course.'

'I'll see you later, then.' His eyes meshed with hers and she read the promise there. Despite all the efforts of her brain to maintain common sense, her heart lurched with excitement. He was definitely telling her that last night hadn't been a one-off for him.

Joy bubbled up inside her and she watched while he left the room and then tried to concentrate on giving the children their breakfast.

'Why are you smiling, Jenny?' Zoe's innocent question made her bite her lip with guilt.

Their mother was lying ill in hospital and here she was smiling like an idiot because of Alex.

'It's always good to try and smile, Zoe,' she said quietly, remembering all the times she'd almost forgotten how to smile after Daisy's birth. 'Do you want some more milk?'

Zoe held out her cup. 'Will I be able to see Mummy today?'

'I hope so.' Jenny poured milk into the cup. 'Your daddy arrived last night so he'll come and see you soon, too.'

'Daddy?' Zoe's face lit up with excitement and she drank her milk while Athena flung a half-eaten bread roll across the kitchen floor.

They spent a quiet morning at home, playing with toys and painting pictures, and halfway through the morning the phone rang in Alex's study.

Jenny hesitated. Should she answer it?

What if it was Andreas, calling from the hospital?

Deciding that she couldn't risk ignoring a phone when Libby was so ill, she checked that the children were occupied and hurried into Alex's study.

The phone stopped ringing as she reached it and she realised that there was a fax coming through.

Relieved that it obviously hadn't been anything to do with Libby, she turned to leave the room but then she recognised her name on the top of the paper.

Feeling vaguely uncomfortable, she reached for the first sheet and saw the bold letterhead of a major London law firm followed by a heading that contained her name.

Hands shaking, she clutched at the paper, reading the report that followed. Her face paled and she sank down onto one of Alex's chairs as she read the detail of the lawyer's investigations.

She was still staring at the paper in mute horror when Zoe pushed her way into the room.

'Daisy's finished her milk and Athena has dripped paint on Uncle Alex's floor,' she said, tilting her head to one side as she looked at Jenny. 'You look sick? Are you sick?'

Jenny struggled to find her voice. 'I'm not sick,' she croaked, standing up with an effort and putting the papers down on Alex's desk. 'I'm fine.'

Considering the fact that she'd just discovered that Alex couldn't possibly be Daisy's father. According to the report, he'd done no more than dance one dance with her sister that night and Chloe had left with someone entirely different. Someone who she'd then spent the night with. A high-profile public figure who was married and already had three children by his very beautiful wife. A man whose marriage was held up as a perfect example of family life.

No wonder Chloe had been reluctant to tell her who the father was.

Jenny covered her eyes with her hands, utterly consumed by the enormity of Chloe's lies.

It was clear now why she'd refused to name the baby's father right through her pregnancy. To have exposed this man would have led to a massive public scandal that would have harmed everyone, including Chloe and her unborn child.

Jenny sucked in a breath.

Had this man ever known about the baby? Had her sister even tried to contact him? Or had he regretted his affair and turned his back on her?

Perhaps she'd never know the answer, but one thing she did know for sure—Alex Westerling was not Daisy's father.

She thought about all the accusations she'd flung at him and gave a groan of horror. How could she have said all those terrible things? And she'd forced herself and Daisy on him, moved into his house, interrupted his life…

She raised a hand to her mouth, totally appalled at her own behaviour.

How could she have done that?

But she knew the answer, of course. She'd believed Chloe. And Chloe, knowing that she was dangerously ill, had obviously wanted to secure protection for Daisy. A mother's instinct to do the best for her child.

But whatever Chloe's motivations had been, the truth

was that Alex had absolutely no responsibility towards Daisy at all and she didn't fool herself that he felt anything for *her* other than lust.

There was no doubt at all that he'd be delighted to receive the lawyer's letter.

'Jenny?'

Realising that Zoe was still looking at her with a worried look on her little face, she forced herself to stand up and walk through to the kitchen, dealing with the children on automatic.

She'd already decided what she must do.

She had to leave.

And she just couldn't face Alex. She'd moved into his house with a baby who wasn't his, had said such dreadful things to him, had believed him capable of—

She closed her eyes briefly and sucked in a breath. As soon as Andreas arrived from the hospital, she'd leave.

And Alex could return to the bachelor existence that he treasured so much.

CHAPTER TEN

ANDREAS arrived towards lunchtime and the girls flung themselves on him with undisguised delight.

Jenny had already packed her little car and had left a short note to Alex. She'd torn up six versions, her brain totally refusing to produce the right words as she'd tried to apologise for the dreadful things she'd said. How did one even begin to apologise for being so completely and utterly wrong?

In the end she'd given up trying to say what was in her heart and had just left a short, succinct letter of apology that stated the facts but left out the emotion.

And now that Andreas had arrived, she could leave.

The prospect left her feeling utterly depressed.

'How is Libby?'

'Much better.' Andreas smiled and Jenny could see immediately why Libby had fallen for him. He was a very charismatic man. 'We hope to bring her home in the morning. In the meantime I'm going to take the girls to see her. She's missing them terribly.'

'And they've missed her.' Jenny gave him a wan smile and Andreas looked at her keenly.

'Is everything all right?' His Greek accent was suddenly very pronounced. 'You look very troubled about something. Have my girls been hard work?'

She shook her head immediately. 'They've been wonderful. I love them.'

It was true. The little girls were completely adorable and they'd been enchanted by Daisy, caring for her as if she were a tiny doll.

Andreas looked at her closely. 'But you are upset about

something—I can see that.' His tone was unbelievably gentle. 'Can I help?'

She shook her head, not trusting herself to speak. His kindness was the final straw. She really had to get away.

'I made some chocolate-chip muffins for Libby,' she muttered, hurrying into the kitchen so that he couldn't see the tears in her eyes. 'She's probably not up to eating yet but I wanted to do something.'

'If it's chocolate, Libby will eat it,' Andreas said dryly, 'and it was very kind of you. But, Jenny—'

'I have to go and see to Daisy,' she said quickly, and without giving him a chance to say more Jenny handed him the tin of cakes and left the room.

Alex checked the monitors and glanced at his sister. 'Everything looks OK.'

'I know that. They've been in here a hundred times to check on me.' Libby looked at him with affection and gratitude. 'I don't know what to say, Alex…'

'Say that from now on you'll carry two adrenaline injections,' Alex drawled, back to his cool self now that his sister was out of danger. 'One wasn't enough.'

Libby closed her eyes at the memory. 'I was *so* scared—I keep remembering—'

'Don't—it was the worse moment of my life.' Alex's voice was suddenly gruff and he leaned forward to hug his sister just as Andreas walked into the room with the children.

There was an emotional reunion and the children totally ignored hospital protocol and crawled all over the bed to get to their mother.

Andreas took his brother-in-law to one side. 'I met Jenny.'

Alex smiled. 'Great, isn't she? Doubtless she was cooking.'

Andreas didn't return the smile. 'Have you spoken to her today?'

Alex frowned slightly, his eyes on his sister. 'Yes—briefly this morning. Why?'

'She looked very upset about something when I arrived,' Andreas said quietly. 'She wouldn't tell me what.'

Alex turned, suddenly giving him his full attention. 'Upset?'

'It was probably nothing.' Andreas shrugged dismissively. 'The children had made a terrible mess—it was probably that.'

'Jenny doesn't care about mess,' Alex said tersely. 'And small children don't faze her in the least. In fact, I haven't really seen anything much faze her.'

Suddenly he felt an intense feeling of foreboding.

'You're sure something was wrong?'

'Well, I don't know her, of course, but, yes…' Andreas lifted a broad shoulder '…I'd say something was very wrong. She looked…stricken.'

Stricken?

After what they'd shared the night before he hadn't expected Jenny to look anything but happy.

But what did you really give her last night? a tiny voice nagged him as he struggled to make sense of his feelings. He wasn't the type of man who said 'I love you', even in the middle of the hottest sex, and he was well aware that he hadn't said it to Jenny. But she hadn't minded that. Had she?

In fact, she'd even told him that she didn't expect commitment.

Which just about made her his perfect woman.

So why was he panicking about losing her?

He'd never worried about losing a woman before. Ever.

Shaken out of his customary cool by emotions he didn't understand, Alex looked at his sister. 'I need to go home. I need to check on Jenny. I'll see you later.'

Libby shifted Athena out of the way so she could concentrate on her brother. 'She loves you, Alex. Really, really loves you.'

Alex tensed, his conscience pricking him for the first time in his life.

Damn. He never ever should have made love to her.

But it had been so perfect…

Suddenly he felt as though he was being suffocated and he left the hospital at a run.

He just had a bad feeling.

He drove at a pace that would have horrified Jenny and the minute he pulled up outside his house he knew that Andreas was right. Something was very wrong.

Her car had gone.

Not even bothering to slam the driver's door, he sprinted into the house, hoping to find some evidence that her absence was just temporary. But he knew that it wasn't and a quick glance into the rooms upstairs confirmed that she'd taken all her things.

It wasn't just her car that had gone.

She'd gone, too.

He checked in the kitchen and saw the note left on the table.

His hands shaking, he ripped open the envelope and read the short letter and then strode through to his study to pick up the fax that she'd mentioned.

He skimmed it quickly, taking in the fact that he wasn't Daisy's father, and then dropped the fax back on his desk and turned the air blue with words that would have horrified his sister.

He should have been relieved to have his innocence confirmed but instead he felt an unfamiliar panic surge inside him.

Jenny had gone.

She'd gone because his lawyer had confirmed that he couldn't be Daisy's father.

And suddenly he realised just how much he'd wanted to be exactly that.

He glanced around him, acknowledging for the first time just how much Jenny had changed his life in the short time since she'd entered it. She'd filled all the empty spaces with her warmth and gentleness and she'd turned his house into a home. Not by her cooking or the way she'd nurtured both him and Daisy, but just by her presence.

And he didn't give a damn whether Daisy was his or not. He wanted them back in his life.

For the first time in his life he'd found a woman that he didn't want to lose.

Alex let out a long breath and realised that if he lost Jenny and Daisy he would have lost everything that was important to him.

Without dwelling on his feelings a moment longer, he strode back to his car and drove at a breakneck speed down the road that led away from the coast. He didn't know where she was heading but he guessed that she would have started on this road and his car was a lot faster than hers.

His shoulders rigid with tension, he shifted gears like a racing driver, peering impatiently along every new stretch of road in the hope of seeing her little red car.

But there was nothing and he started to wonder whether he could have been wrong about the direction she'd taken.

Maybe she'd stayed in the village after all, or maybe she'd taken back roads.

Growling with frustration, he was about to hit the accelerator once more when he saw a flash of red up ahead.

He slowed his pace and then felt a lurch of horror.

The flash of red wasn't on the road.

There was a car lying in the ditch, and it was Jenny's.

He hit the brakes and the car came to a halt with a shriek of tyres.

'Jenny!' His voice was hoarse as he slid down the bank to the driver's side. 'Jenny, sweetheart!'

She was slumped against the steering-wheel, eyes closed, blood pouring from a cut on her head.

Glancing into the back seat, Alex saw that Daisy was still safely strapped in her car seat and was crying noisily.

She seemed to be OK, which was more than could be said for Jenny.

Panic pulsing through his veins for the second time in twenty-four hours, he fumbled for his mobile phone and rang for an ambulance, his voice shaking as he gave their position, all the while tugging at the door which had obviously become jammed in the accident.

Ordering them to bring a fire crew as well, he tried the other side of the car and managed to get the door open.

With a rush of relief he slid into the passenger seat. 'Jenny. Jenny, it's Alex. Talk to me.'

He lifted a hand to her neck, checking for a pulse, and then heard the sound of a siren.

He checked her airway, satisfied himself that it was clear and that she was breathing, and did a quick assessment of the rest of her injuries. She didn't appear to be bleeding anywhere apart from the cut on her head and he could see her feet and legs.

Then he leaned into the back seat and swiftly checked Daisy.

'Well, at least you're crying, angel, which means you're conscious,' he said softly, checking her as best he could while she was still in her car seat.

'Alex?' The face of one of the paramedics appeared at the window and he turned with relief.

'Mike, get the baby out of here—and be careful with her. I think she's all right but I can't be sure. Then get back here with a backboard. Jenny might have hurt her neck.'

There was no way he was going to risk moving Jenny without some sort of support to her cervical spine.

As the fire engine arrived, Jenny opened her eyes.

'Jenny!' Alex's voice was hoarse and he stroked a gentle hand over her head. 'Sweetheart, can you hear me?'

Her eyes drifted closed again and he fought against the panic that rose inside him.

'Jenny!'

She opened her eyes again and looked at him. 'Daisy?'

He let out a groan of relief at her croaked question. At least she could remember something about what had happened.

It was typical of Jenny that her first thought was for Daisy.

'Daisy's fine and we're going to get you out of this car really soon. We're just fetching a backboard.'

'My head hurts.'

'Anything else? Does it hurt anywhere else?'

His tone was urgent and there was a brief pause while she thought about his question. 'No. I don't think so.'

The next half-hour was a blur of frantic activity while everyone worked to free Jenny from the car.

Finally she was in the ambulance and Alex scrambled in beside her. 'OK. *Move!*'

Jenny looked at him, her face bruised and battered. 'You can't leave your precious car by the side of the road— someone might drive into it.'

'I don't care about my car.' He took her hand in his. 'Jenny, do you remember what happened?'

She didn't appear to be suffering from memory loss but she'd been knocked out and he wanted to check.

'I remember.' She closed her eyes and then they fluttered open again. 'How did you know where to find me?'

He gave a wan smile. 'Lucky guess. What happened? Why did you crash?'

Her eyes slid away from his. 'I don't know. I suppose I wasn't concentrating.'

His grip tightened on her hand. 'All right. Don't worry

about that now. The only thing that matters is that you're both OK.'

And, thank God, they seemed to be.

He just wanted to get her to the unit so that he could check that she hadn't done any damage to her cervical spine.

'Alex—' her voice was a croak '—did you get my letter?'

His jaw clenched. 'Yes.'

'She isn't yours.' Her eyes filled. 'I really believed she was. I'm so sorry for everything I said.'

His body tensed and he fought the impulse to drag her roughly into his arms and kiss her senseless. He didn't want to risk making her injuries worse and anyway they had a paramedic sitting in the back with them.

'We can't talk about this now,' he said gruffly, squeezing her hand to reassure her. 'Wait till we've sorted you out then we've got all the time in the world to talk.'

'But—'

'Later,' he said, glancing impatiently out of the window. 'Where the hell are we?'

'Nearly there,' the paramedic said quietly, and sure enough Alex recognised the entrance to the hospital.

He just wanted to arrive so that he could give Jenny and Daisy a thorough check-up.

And then they had some serious talking to do.

Jenny lay in the bed with Daisy in a cot next to her.

'Do I really have to stay in overnight?' she asked the nurse, who was checking her blood pressure yet again.

'You had a nasty bump on the head,' the nurse reminded her, recording the results with a satisfied nod. 'Fortunately everything seems to be all right but Alex will hang us out to dry if we let you move a muscle before he says so.'

Jenny gave a weak smile. 'He's a bully.'

'That's me.' His dark drawl came from the doorway and

he took the chart from the nurse and glanced at the monitors. 'How are you feeling?'

Jenny pulled a face. 'Headache, but apart from that—fine.'

'Have you been sick?'

She shook her head. 'I'm all right. Really.'

'Well, we're keeping you in to be on the safe side.' He rolled his eyes. 'What with you and Libby, we can virtually fill a ward with our family.'

Our family.

The words caused a pain so intense that she closed her eyes. They reminded her of just how desperately she'd wanted to be just that.

A family.

With Alex.

Somehow she'd got used to living with him. Even though she'd always known that there could never be anything permanent between them, she'd played the role so convincingly for Daisy's sake that now she was finding it hard to let go of the dream.

Alex looked at her stricken face and turned to the nurse. 'Can you leave us, please?'

She vanished immediately, closing the door behind her.

'Right.' Alex sat on the bed, his handsome face inscrutable as ever. 'Time for you and I to have a chat.'

'Yes.' She pinned a smile on her face, knowing what was coming. He wanted an apology. 'I just don't know how to apologise for what I said to you—all the things I accused you of. There's nothing I can say, except that I was so wrong about you.'

'Only about Daisy's paternity,' Alex said flatly, all traces of humour totally absent. 'You were pretty much right about everything else. I am a selfish, thoughtless bastard.'

Jenny stared at him, startled.

She'd expected him to be condemning *her*, not himself.

'That's not true and you know it,' she said softly. 'You're incredibly generous.'

He gave a wry smile. 'I think you've painted a rather glossy picture of me, sweetheart.'

Looking at the slightly tousled dark hair, the rough jaw and the devilish blue eyes, Jenny failed to see how any picture of Alex Westerling could ever come near to doing him justice, let alone be too glossy.

'Did you read the fax?'

She was still reeling with shock at the discovery of Daisy's true paternity and Alex's mouth tightened.

'Yes.' He gave a short laugh. 'What are you going to do?'

Jenny shook her head and turned to look at Daisy who was sleeping contentedly. 'I've decided not to do anything.'

Alex's mouth tightened. 'He owes you some sort of support.'

She turned back to him, her smile sad. 'He's married with three children, Alex. The only support he'd be able to give us is financial and I don't need that. What I really want for Daisy is a loving father. A good man in her life. Every little girl should have that.'

Alex sucked in a breath. 'So you're going to let him off?'

'It isn't an easy decision, but I'm thinking of his family rather than him,' Jenny said softly. 'How can I approach him, knowing that it could ruin his marriage and have dreadful consequences for his children? I'm pretty sure that what he and Chloe shared was just a one-night thing—a mistake for both of them.'

Alex took her hands in his. 'You're so damned forgiving.' He stroked a thumb over the palm of her hand, seeming strangely hesitant for once in his life.

'Well, after last night I'm not quite so naïve about sex,' Jenny confessed, a rueful smile touching her soft mouth. 'I can see how people might be swept away by the excitement. Common sense can go out of the window, even for a one-night stand.'

How could she condemn Chloe when she herself had followed the intensity of her emotions the night before?

'A one-night stand?' Alex's tone was hoarse. 'Is that what you think last night was for us?'

She blushed slightly and tried to tug her hand away from his, but he held it firmly. 'Alex, I know what sort of man you are. I know about your three-month rule.'

'I've always believed that rules are there to be broken.' Alex's voice was rough and his hands tightened on hers. 'Jenny, I need to tell you a few things about myself. Things I've never shared with anyone apart from my sisters.'

She lay still, hardly daring to breathe, wondering what was coming. It was so unlike Alex to talk about himself. And it was obviously a struggle for him.

'My parents had the worst marriage you can imagine,' he said flatly. 'They fought, argued and my father had a string of very public affairs which my mother chose to ignore.'

Jenny held onto his hand. 'And you witnessed it all?'

'Fortunately the girls and I were sent to boarding school from a very young age.'

Fortunately?

Her heart contracted as she imagined what it must have been like for a small boy to be sent away from home. Away from all family contact. 'That must have been awful for you.'

'Awful?' He gave a bitter laugh. 'Actually, it was an escape from hell. It was the holidays that were awful but I usually managed to wangle myself an invite to a friend's house.'

Jenny looked at him helplessly. No wonder he was so fiercely independent. He'd been managing on his own from an age when most children were still utterly dependent on their parents.

'Is that the reason you've never wanted to commit to one woman?' she asked softly. 'Because you think that all marriages are like your parents'?'

He shook his head. 'No. I know that all marriages aren't like that. Libby and Katy are prime examples. They're both crazily in love with their respective partners. I just never thought that marriage was for me. Before today I never saw the point, to be honest. I always believed that marriage just forces people to stay together, who shouldn't be together, and sometimes children are caught in the crossfire.'

Before today?

What did he mean, before today?

Squashing down the tiny bud of hope which started to bloom inside her, Jenny hardly dared to breathe. 'What's different today?'

Alex released her hands and cupped her face, looking deep into her eyes. 'Today,' he said softly, 'was the day you tried to drive out of my life. Today was the day that I finally understood why people get married. Today I finally discovered what people mean by the word "love". It's what I feel for you, Red Riding Hood.'

Jenny stared at him, mute. He couldn't be saying what she thought he was saying. She must have misunderstood. 'Alex?'

Her voice was a wistful croak and he lowered his head and kissed her gently on her parted lips. 'Jenny, I want to be that man in Daisy's life. And I want to be the man in your life. One night isn't enough, and three months won't be either.'

She stared at him. He wanted Daisy? He wanted her?

'Are you going to say something?' His blue gaze was suddenly intense. 'Last night you said you loved me, Jenny. Did you mean it? Do you mean it enough to marry me?'

She ran a tongue over her dry lips. 'You want to marry me?'

He gave a wry smile. 'I never thought I'd have to say

the words twice. There's arrogance for you. Yes, I want to marry you. I want to marry you because there is no damn way I'm letting another man lay a finger on you. Last night I made you mine and I intend to keep you as mine. You let the wolf into your life and now there's no escape.'

Swamped by a cloud of euphoria, Jenny smiled. It seemed too much like a fantasy to be real and she couldn't quite let herself believe it.

Did real life really have endings like this?

'You really want to marry me?' She bit her lip and looked up at him. 'I disrupted your bachelor lifestyle.'

'Totally.'

'I make you eat breakfast '

His eyes dropped to her mouth. 'I love your breakfast.'

'I hide your whisky.'

His blue eyes gleamed. 'I never thought I'd say this, but I've discovered that there's something I prefer to single malt.'

She blushed. 'Alex…'

'I wonder if eventually you'll stop blushing,' he mused, stroking her cheek with a gentle finger. 'Maybe after fifty years with me you'll have got used to my wolfish ways.'

Her eyes twinkled. 'I haven't said yes yet.'

He grinned, his mouth hovering a breath away from hers. 'But you will.'

'You're very sure of yourself, Dr Westerling,' she whispered, feeling her heart rate increase dramatically. 'What if I say no?'

'I don't understand the word no,' he groaned, leaning forward to claim her mouth in a gentle kiss. 'I had a very limited education.'

'I can't believe you truly want the two of us.'

'Well, I do. And I'll do my best to be the very best father to Daisy. I know I've been pretty wild in the past, but you calm me down, Jen. I can learn the father stuff.'

She lifted a hand and touched his cheek. 'I never had

any doubts that you'd be a brilliant father. It was only ever you who believed that.'

'Because I didn't think I could commit to anyone,' he said, 'and I wasn't willing to risk bringing children into a doomed relationship.'

'And now?' She gazed up at him. 'Do you believe you'll be a good father now?'

'With you as the mother, definitely,' he groaned, kissing her until the room started to spin. 'If I step out of line, you'll soon tell me. And now do you think you could put a chap out of his misery and give me an answer? Will you marry me or are you going to load up your basket of bread rolls and go back into the forest to search for Grandma?'

'She lived in the cottage,' Jenny reminded him, and his broad shoulders lifted in a shrug.

'See? I'm really going to need your help to do the daddy stuff properly. So what do you say?'

'Yes.' What other answer could there possibly be but yes? 'Very yes.'

He grinned. 'Very yes?'

'Very, very yes.'

'In that case you might want to wear this, just in case any of those doctors who keep slinking into your room to check up on you get any funny ideas.' He slid a hand into the pocket of his trousers and withdrew a tiny box which he flipped open.

Jenny gasped as she saw the beautiful diamond ring. 'That's for me?'

'Unless you want Daisy to have it.'

'B-but when did you get a chance to buy it?' Suddenly she couldn't bear the fact that he might have chosen this ring for someone else.

'I bullied the jeweller's into opening early for me,' Alex said, slipping the ring onto her finger. 'I know what you're thinking, but I've never bought a ring for anyone else in my life, angel—trust me on that one. This is just for you.'

Just for her?

Jenny stared down at her finger and her eyes filled. 'This is like a fairy-tale.'

'Not exactly,' Alex mocked gently. 'In the fairy-tale it wasn't the wolf who ended up with Red Riding Hood.'

She gave him a watery smile. 'I always thought the wolf was terribly misunderstood.'

Alex gave her a smile that was totally male. 'I wouldn't be so sure about that.'

And he bent his head and kissed her.

EPILOGUE

THE garden party was in full swing. An army of waiters circulated with champagne and the guests mingled in groups on the lawn.

'I cannot believe that Dad agreed to a bouncy castle,' Alex drawled, watching with amusement as the children slithered and jumped, shrieking with delight.

'He didn't.' Libby smiled smugly at her brother. 'I ordered it. My two absolutely adore bouncy castles and I didn't see why they shouldn't enjoy the party. It's more than we ever did as children. I arranged for it to arrive a few hours ago so Dad didn't have time to protest.'

Alex laughed and then glanced down to find Daisy tugging at his trouser leg. 'Hello, my angel.' He scooped her up in his arms and planted a kiss on her cheek. 'Having fun?'

'She's gorgeous, Alex.' Libby smiled as she looked at the little girl. 'I can't believe she's two and a half. Just think, it's been two whole years since I first met her. Remember my bee sting? It was so awful.'

Alex lifted an eyebrow. 'Bee sting? What bee sting?' But despite his mocking tone, his gaze was soft as it rested on his sister. 'I assume you carry adrenaline?'

Libby nodded and patted her handbag. 'Of course. Andreas is utterly paranoid about it. He has stocks of it everywhere.'

'Good.' Alex glanced across the lawn and grimaced. 'Have you seen Athena? What *has* she been eating this time?'

Libby smiled happily. 'Ketchup. Andreas banned it but she smiled at one of the waiters and he found her a giant bottle. I just stopped her wiping her fingers on the Prime Minister's jacket.'

'A Prime Minister with "red" streaks,' Alex said, his blue eyes amused. 'An interesting political statement.'

Libby looked from him to Daisy. 'It's been two years, Alex. Are you ever going to tell us who her real father is?'

Alex tensed and his blue eyes hardened. 'I'm her father,' he said softly, holding the little girl more tightly. 'She's my baby girl, aren't you, sweetheart?'

He nuzzled her neck and Daisy chuckled happily just as Jenny arrived looking cool and pretty in a blue linen dress.

'You look great in that colour,' Libby said warmly, 'and those shoes look fantastic with that dress.'

Jenny glanced down at herself and smiled shyly. 'It was kind of you to lend them to me. I'm being really careful how I walk. I'm not used to heels this high. I'm afraid I'll fracture something. On the other hand, it is nice not to feel so small compared to Alex.' She turned to him with an awed expression on her face. 'Did you know that Libby has *sixty-three* pairs of shoes?'

Alex yawned. 'Is that all? She's obviously sold some of them then.'

Libby laughed and thumped him on the shoulder. 'Vile man. It's just as well you have Jenny to reform you.'

Alex's eyes gleamed as they rested on his wife. 'Reform me?' He stepped closer to Jenny, enjoying her soft blush. 'I don't think so.'

'Alex!' Jenny backed away and glanced round self-consciously. 'I don't want to shock your father.'

'Oh, but I do,' Libby said happily. 'It's my favourite pastime. Go ahead. Shock away.'

'Don't start, Lib.' Katy joined them, holding the hands of her two seven-year-old boys. 'Dad is so much better. He's trying really hard to relax.' She turned to Jenny. 'Where are your twins?'

'With Andreas and Jago,' Jenny said, pointing across the lawn. 'They're using them as a climbing frame.'

Katy laughed. 'Isn't it amazing? Two sets of twin boys in the family.'

Alex reached out a hand and pulled Jenny towards him in a totally male gesture of possession. 'Actually, I would have rather had them separately.' He dropped a gentle kiss on Jenny's head. 'I worried about you right the way through your pregnancy. You seem too delicate to carry one baby safely, let alone two.'

Jenny gazed up at him lovingly and Libby and Katy melted into the background with knowing smiles.

Jenny and Alex found themselves on their own with Daisy.

'So…' His voice was husky and so sexy that it made her nerve endings tingle. 'Do you fancy slipping away somewhere more private?'

Jenny's eyes widened. 'Alex, we can't.'

He gave a slow smile. 'You've been married to me for almost two years, Jen. I've given you two babies. How can you still blush?'

'It's you!' She bit her lip and looked away, flustered, 'You always make me feel—feel…'

'Yes?' He stepped closer again, this time not giving her the chance to back away. 'How do I make you feel?'

Staring into his wicked blue eyes, Jenny felt her stomach drop away. 'Oh, Alex, I love you so much.'

He sucked in a breath and stooped to put Daisy on the ground. 'Sweetheart, go and play with your cousin Zoe for five minutes.'

Daisy ran off happily and Alex followed her with his eyes for a few seconds, checking that she was safe. Then he turned his attention back to his wife.

'Come with me.'

He took her hand and walked along a path that wound its way away from the guests towards an ornamental lake.

'Where are we going?'

'Somewhere more private.' Alex flashed her a smile. 'Since I'm aware that you don't like public displays of affection.'

They reached the lake and he hauled her into the shade of a weeping willow.

'Now, then, Jenny Westerling.' His voice was loaded with promise and he pushed her against the tree trunk, blocking her escape. 'What were you saying about loving me?'

She gave a moan and lifted her mouth for his kiss.

Heat flared between them and Jenny wrapped her slim arms around his neck, trembling as he deepened the kiss.

When he finally lifted his head, neither of them was smiling. 'Damn.' His voice was husky. 'Let's go home.'

Still in the grip of sizzling sexual attraction, Jenny stared at him stupidly. 'Alex we can't.'

'Jenny, I want you. Now.' He stroked her hair away from her face with a hand that was far from steady. 'We either leave, or we make love here and risk an audience. Your choice.'

Her knees were shaking. 'Alex, the children—'

'Will be more than happy to leave, too,' he said gently. 'Believe me, Dad isn't going to notice whether we're here or not. He's too busy networking. Frankly I'd rather get home to the cottage where I can rip that dress off you and do what I've been longing to do since we left Cornwall this morning.'

Jenny blushed. 'Alex, it's only been about eight hours since we—' She broke off, thoroughly embarrassed, and his blue eyes gleamed with amusement.

'Yes, angel? Since we…?'

Jenny looked at him helplessly. It didn't matter how often they made love, she still wanted him with a desperation that shocked her.

'I love you, Alex,' she breathed, and he gave a groan and lowered his head to hers.

'And I love you, sweetheart. More than anything in the world. Let's go home.'

And they did…

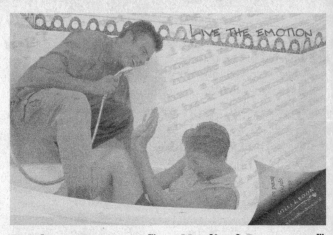

Modern Romance™
...international affairs
– seduction and
passion guaranteed

Medical Romance™
...pulse-raising
romance – heart-
racing medical drama

Tender Romance™
...sparkling, emotional,
feel-good romance

Sensual Romance™
...teasing, tempting,
provocatively playful

Historical Romance™
...rich, vivid and
passionate

Blaze Romance™
...scorching hot
sexy reads

27 new titles every month.

Live the emotion

MILLS & BOON®

MB4

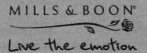

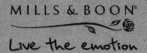

MILLS & BOON®

Live the emotion

Medical Romance™

THE CONSULTANT'S ACCIDENTAL BRIDE
by Carol Marinelli *A&E Drama*

An accident forces emergency nurse Leah Jacobs to share a home with A&E consultant Cole Richardson. His ice-cool reserve is driving her mad, but the drama and emotion of A&E give her a glimpse of his tender side. And then a major incident brings back memories that Cole has buried deep inside…

THE REGISTRAR'S SECRET **by Judy Campbell**

Dr Emma Fulford was determined to be relationship-free – so she didn't expect to fall for the infuriatingly attractive Dr Sean Casey. But when the two registrars had to work side by side in the hustle and bustle of A&E, there was no way they could ignore the sparks flying between them!

CHALLENGING DR CARLISLE **by Joanna Neil**

Dr Sarah Carlisle is in love with the wrong man – her boss! How can she care for someone who abandoned her sister when pregnant? Working with the devilishly sexy Dr Matthew Bayford is a challenge, but soon Sarah discovers he isn't as off-limits as she thought. Her sister's baby isn't his, for a start…

On sale 4th June 2004

Available at most branches of WHSmith, Tesco, Martins, Borders, Eason, Sainsbury's and all good paperback bookshops.

0504/03b

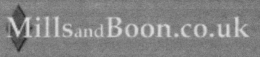

FREE!

4 Books
and a surprise gift!

We would like to take this opportunity to thank you for reading this Mills & Boon® book by offering you the chance to take FOUR more specially selected titles from the Medical Romance™ series absolutely FREE! We're also making this offer to introduce you to the benefits of the Reader Service™—

★ FREE home delivery
★ FREE gifts and competitions
★ FREE monthly Newsletter
★ Books available before they're in the shops
★ Exclusive Reader Service discount

Accepting these FREE books and gift places you under no obligation to buy; you may cancel at any time, even after receiving your free shipment. Simply complete your details below and return the entire page to the address below. *You don't even need a stamp!*

YES! Please send me 4 free Medical Romance books and a surprise gift. I understand that unless you hear from me, I will receive 6 superb new titles every month for just £2.69 each, postage and packing free. I am under no obligation to purchase any books and may cancel my subscription at any time. The free books and gift will be mine to keep in any case.

M4ZEE

Ms/Mrs/Miss/Mr ....Initials...
BLOCK CAPITALS PLEASE

Surname...

Address...

....

....Postcode ....

Send this whole page to:
UK: The Reader Service, FREEPOST CN81, Croydon, CR9 3WZ
EIRE: The Reader Service, PO Box 4546, Kilcock, County Kildare (stamp required)